TRIAL OF MISFORTUNE

PATLOLLA AKSHAINIE REDDY

Made with ❤ on the Notion Press Platform
www.notionpress.com

To my Mom & Dad.

Anddd to my brother and my dog >3

Contents

Contents

Acknowledgements

First and foremost, big shoutout to my dog for keeping me company during those long writing sessions. Your happy tail wags and soulful eyes were the perfect motivation to keep me going, even when the words just wouldn't flow.

. . .

To my mom, thanks for pretending to understand what my book is about, even though I'm pretty sure you stopped listening after I mentioned talking monkeys. Your unwavering support means the world to me, even if you still think I should have done my homework.

. . .

To my dad, whose sage writing advice and unwavering support propelled me through the toughest chapters. Your words of wisdom were like guiding lights in the dark tunnel of creativity, always leading me towards the perfect plot twist. Thanks for always reminding me that every story has its own **campaign** trail.

. . .

And to my annoying younger brother, thanks for constantly barging into my room just when I was on the brink of a breakthrough. Your impeccable timing truly deserves an award, preferably one that comes with noise-canceling headphones.

. . .

To my friends, thanks for not giving up on me when I disappeared into my writing cave for months on end. Your texts about random conspiracy theories and dog memes kept me sane (well, relatively speaking).

. . .

Huge shoutout to coffee and chocolate for being my constant companions on this literary journey. I couldn't have done it without your caffeine-fueled inspiration and sugar-induced motivation.

...

To my computer, thank you for not crashing (most of the time) and for miraculously saving my work when I forgot to hit save for the hundredth time. You're the real MVP.

...

Last but not least, to anyone who actually reads this book, whether by choice or because your English teacher made you, I owe you a virtual high-five and a lifetime supply of imaginary tacos. Thanks for giving my words a home in your brain.

...

And to anyone I forgot to mention, blame it on the caffeine withdrawal-induced brain fog. You know who you are.

...

(My mom made me write this) I'm not actually allowed coffee. Reach for your dreams, right? :)

Foreword

In the pages that follow, you will embark on an extraordinary journey alongside Autumn, a 15-year-old girl whose life takes a tragic turn when she loses her mother during a family trip. What begins as a tale of loss and grief swiftly transforms into a gripping saga of resilience, friendship, and determination against all odds.

As Autumn delves into the dark depths of the Los Zetas tribe, uncovering secrets that shatter her understanding of her own past, she finds herself thrust into a world of danger and intrigue. Alongside her long-lost cousin Antonio, she navigates treacherous terrain, facing adversaries both human and elemental.

Their odyssey leads them to unlikely allies, including the kind-hearted Lena who's capabilities are endless, and the enigmatic Jameson, whose icy exterior belies a complex inner world. Together, they forge bonds that transcend borders and cultures, united in their quest for freedom and justice.

But theirs is not a journey without sacrifice. Along the way, they encounter Ammorette, a soul scarred by the cruelty of fate, and Antonio, driven by a thirst for truth that takes him down a path of uncertainty and danger.

As you turn the pages of this gripping narrative, prepare to be swept away by a tale of courage, hope, and the enduring power of the human spirit. For within these words lie not just the story of one girl's quest for redemption, but a testament to the resilience of the human heart in the face of adversity.

Welcome to the world of Autumn, where every twist and turn brings new revelations and challenges, and where the bonds of friendship are forged in the fires of adversity. Enjoy the journey, for this is only the beginning.

. . .

Patlolla Akshainie Reddy.

Preface

In crafting the tale you are about to embark upon, I was driven by a singular desire: to weave a narrative that transcends the ordinary, transporting readers to a world where the boundaries between reality and imagination blur and where the human spirit shines brightest in the darkest of times.

The story of Autumn, her companions, and their perilous journey from the heart of Mexico to the bustling streets of London is not merely a work of fiction; it is a tapestry of emotions, experiences, and universal truths woven together with threads of adventure, mystery, and hope.

The challenges faced by our heroes as they bravely and tenaciously take on their inner demons and external foes are echoes of real-world battles and victories found inside these pages. Their journey, which takes them from the lowest points of loss and sadness to the highest points of friendship and camaraderie, speaks to the complexity of the human experience.

I want you to suspend disbelief and enjoy the magic of storytelling as you set out on this journey with Autumn and her friends. Let the currents of fate and fortune carry you away, and you'll find a mirror of your own hopes, anxieties, and dreams in these pages.

Ultimately, Autumn's tale is not just hers; it is a story that we all own, serving as a reminder of the value of friendship, the strength of tenacity, and the limitless potential that each and every one of us possesses.

So I'm inviting you to turn the page and come along on an adventure that won't be like any other, dear reader. Because there is a world of wonder and adventure waiting to be discovered and experienced within these words.

...

Patolla Akshainie Reddy

Prologue

In the shadowed depths of a moonlit forest, where ancient trees whispered secrets to the night sky, a young girl named Autumn stood alone, her heart heavy with grief and uncertainty. The events of the past days had unfolded like a nightmare, leaving her world shattered and her soul adrift on a sea of sorrow.

It had begun with a family trip, a journey filled with laughter and anticipation, until tragedy struck with the suddenness of a lightning bolt. In the blink of an eye, her mother was gone, stolen from her by a cruel twist of fate. And in the aftermath of her loss, Autumn found herself thrust into a world of danger and darkness, where the boundaries between reality and nightmare blurred.

For in the wake of her mother's death, secrets long buried began to surface, revealing a tangled web of deception and betrayal. A tribe known as the Los Zetas loomed on the periphery of her existence, their presence casting a shadow of fear and uncertainty over her life. And as she delved deeper into the mysteries of her past, Autumn uncovered truths that threatened to unravel the very fabric of her existence.

But amidst the chaos and despair, a glimmer of hope emerged—a chance encounter with a long-lost cousin, a beacon of light in the darkness. Together, they embarked on a perilous journey, determined to uncover the truth behind their family's fate and to forge a path to redemption.

And so, as the moon cast its silver glow upon the forest floor, Autumn took her first tentative steps into the unknown, her heart filled with both fear and determination. For she knew that the road ahead would be fraught with danger and uncertainty, but she also knew that she would not walk it alone.

For Autumn was not just a girl grieving the loss of her mother; she was a survivor, a warrior, destined for greatness in a world teetering on the edge of chaos. And as she stood beneath the stars, her gaze fixed on the horizon, she knew that her journey was only just beginning.

The tale of Autumn was about to unfold—a tale of loss and love, of darkness and light, of courage and redemption. And as the first whispers of dawn began to stir the sleeping world, she took her first step into destiny's embrace, ready to face whatever challenges lay ahead.

For she was Autumn, and her story was just beginning...

1

Choosing.

Look, I'm practically dead.

My five senses are not working, but unfortunately, my heart still is. And my survival instincts are too

Strong. Curse you dad. I'm a pro at swimming, but my body is not working, my *mind* is not working.

A splash of water on my face wakes me up.

No. Wait.

I'm not dreaming. My head is going in and out of the water, my eyes burning. I lunge for a floating piece of

bark, I can see Bronwyn. My eyes go wide, and everything slow-motion. He's kicking and flailing, he can't

swim. Dad is trying to reach him but he's stuck, with one final roar of frustration he lunges toward

Bronwyn only to be pulled back, and the sound of the splash drowned by Bronwyn's gurgling cries. I see

mom, her orange hair is floating in the water like some kind of demented octupus. But she's long gone. I

will myself desperately not to look in her direction, and gulp back tears. Her locket is floating in the water

innocently. I made a grab for it, shoved into my pocket as far as it would go. I'm not sure of what's happening. A childish scream is drowned under the roar of a waterfall. I pant, breath labored, Bronwyn

briefly makes eye contact with me, his eyes, big and wet. And I dive under, swimming to Bronwyn. I

grab his arms and yanked hard. Pulling each other under the water I manage to lug him along and dump

him on shore. I can't leave Dad. I look him in the eyes, he looks back. A longing sad look in his eyes. "Go!"

he manages to choke out. I look at him cluelessly, "The tides rising, go! I won't make it!"

Its' times like this when I don't think. When I don't have the capacity to think.

Its life or death.

I choose death.

2

The Waters's Second Attempt at Murder

The saltwater is burning my eyes, but I can see. I can see Dad's leg, I can see the seaweed. I can see

The knife in my hand. I can see my hand, working with the seaweed. But I can't see myself coming

Up for air. One. Last. Time. Dad's hand yanks me up and the 3 of us doggy paddle to the cave. Not

Seeing, not feeling, not breathing.

. . .

About who – knows – how – many – days later. All of us are conscious. We're still stuck in that cave.

No food. "What should we do?" I ask dad, walking toward him. "I'm not sure, Autumn." He says

Peering at the water, which is now gently caressing our feet. Pft. We're not that stupid, we know

How many people you've killed, Water. "If we make it to the other side, one of us to die." He says

Eventually. "But-" I started, "If I get you both over there I have to die, if we both want to go, we have

To leave Bronze." Bronze was what Mom called Bronwyn. She said dad was her gold, I was her silver,

And Bronwyn was her bronze. "There's a waterfall on the other side, y' know?" he asked me, turning

His head to look at me, squinting. "Dad," I said placing my hand on his arm, "please, let's try, let's do

Something." "You're brave kiddo," he said, giving me a smile, "but I'm not. Not anymore, at least."

The sun is setting, it's a beautiful sight. And we retreat to the back of our cave.

The next morning we're up before sunrise and Bronwyn is hungry. We're all hungry, but for different

Things. Bronwyn wants coconuts. There is a coconut tree right there, but it's risky. We haven't had

Anything to eat in a day, now. "Dad, don't go. Don't be brave if you're not." I pleaded with Dad.

"Otter," that was dad's nickname for me, "please love. This is our only chance of survival." "And your

Death!" I scream in his face. "I will throw the coconuts at you." He said ignoring what I said before,

Glaring at the water. "Catch them. I will be back, I love you, Otter." And with that, I had to let go of

His hand. With a stick in his hand, he carefully made it to the tree, he threw me 6 coconuts. I caught

All of them. And then he slipped, and the current picked up, and this stick broke. "Daddy!" I

shrieked, Bronwyn started crying. The tide picked up even more. With a look of strain on his face

Dad grabbed the stem of the tree with both hands. The current became faster. One hand loose.

"Dad no! Please dad!" I shrieked both my hands on the sides of my head, tears were falling fast.

The current slowed, but only a little. Dad took the opportunity and threw his body in the direction of

The cave. Landing hard on the stone floor. I was immediately by his side. “Dad, are you okay? I told

You not to go!” I practically screamed, hot tears falling on the cave floor, mixing with the sea water.

My fists balled, my body stiff. Dad smiled, he winced as he got up and drew me in close for a hug.

“I’m sorry for scaring you.” He groaned, still smiling. “Coconut?” Bronwyn asked. “Coconut. Coconut.

Coconut. cOConUt!!” Bronwyn demanded, “Alright buddy.” Dad said rubbing his hands together.

We cut open the coconuts with my knife, drank its drinkable water, ate its sweet meat and kept the

Shells just in case. That night, me and dad sat together, leaning on each other against the moonlight.

Our silhouettes cast a ghostly glow. “We’re getting out of here tomorrow,” Dad mumbled.

“How?” I asked, his eyes twinkled, unmoving. “We’re taking the waterfall.”

3

'We're Taking The Waterfall.'

We're all up before the sun's up. But it's the wrong time, the tide's high, the moon is still out.

So we sit, and we wait. And we think, and we regret, and we feel. Finally, we feel the warm glow of

The sun on our faces and dad gets up. He goes to the back of the cave and retrieves a long rope.

"I'm gonna tie this around our waists, so we don't get separated." Sounds good enough. We scale

Some rocks, trees, dragging Bronwyn around and we reach the top of the waterfall. The tide is low.

"When I saw 3, we jump." Dad says, casually looking over the 60ft drop. I nod, then I stop, I stare at

Dad. "Wait, what? Do you plan on committing suicide?" I ask him, he looks at me hard, hands on his

Hips. "Hold my hand from behind Bronwyn. Hold Bronwyn's hands from the front." He instructs.

Bronwyn is whimpering. "Dada." He whines. "It's gonna be okay, Bron." I reassure him. "On three."

Dad says, checking the rope and firmly nodding. "1." This can't be happening. "2" my heart is gonna

Come out of my chest. "3" none of us jump. "I love you guys." Dad says, and we jump. The wind is

Whistling in my ears. Bronwyn is screaming, I'm screaming, we're all crying, suspended in mid-air.

Our hands are not holding each other, they're in the sky streaking behind us like they're gonna fly

off. Finally, we hit the water with a deafening splash.

I crawled out of the water as quickly as possible, I collapse on the land, my whole body shaking from

The adrenaline. And then I slowly roll over to my side, choking out water. And then, I pass out.

4

The Tribe

The first thing I see when I wake up are eyes, greyish blue eyes. I gasp and scramble away. Only to

Find that I'm on a soft mattress. A guy stares at me, he looks older than me by about my age, older.

We stare at each other. "Uh... hi?" I say awkwardly, "Hi." He extends his hand and I shake it. "Nice

to meet you. I'm Antonio. Antonio Yatzil. I'm Jefe Yatzil's son." He says, "Jefe?" I ask, "Chief." He says

Handing me a glass of water, I grab it from his hand and pour it down my throat. I'm gasping and

Panting by the time I'm done. He's staring at me like I'm mad, "What?" I ask, "I haven't had water in

3 days. Or probably more." He laughs, he sounds Mexican. And I smile. Which quickly turns into a

Frown. "Where am I?" I ask him. "Mexico, Tamaulipas. You are in the territory of the Los Zetas tribe.

Jefe Yatzil is our leader." That didn't sound like a piece of information, it sounded like a warning. I

Nod slowly, "Where's dad? Where's my little brother?" he beckons for me to follow him and I do. He leads me to a different area, where dad is eating roasted meat and looking at a man with a weird

headpiece, who is holding a spear and a piece of meat. Bronwyn is playing with some other kids.

I'm guessing that's the chief, the Jefe himself. Jefe Yatzil.

I walk over to dad, bending down to whisper in his ear, "Dad, what are you doing? This is the Los

Zetas tribe. Who do you think they are?! They're dangerous. We have to leave, immediately."

I go to Bronwyn and swiftly pick him up, "Ot!" he exclaims, I give him a firm smile, and walk back

To the campfire. "Dad-" I start but I'm interrupted by the Jefe. "Autumn? Is it?" he asks.

His voice is cold, hard, commanding, and demanding at the same time. "No." what? "Autumn is not

My name." what did just say? My 6th sense, my common sense, was asking me to lie. The Jefe

Raised one eyebrow, and shifted his weight. "Oh? Is it? What is your name then?" I looked around,

And then I looked straight into the Jefe's eyes, "My name is Yvette. Yvette Whitlock. My brothers

Name is Atlas Whitlock and my father's name is Gatsby Whitlock." The chief looks uncertainly from

Me to dad. "I was... told, otherwise little girl. I was told your name is Autumn, your brothers

Bronwyn. And your dad's Alex." He says gesturing vividly to each of us. I frown, "I don't know why

My dad felt the need to lie to you, Jefe Yatzil." I said firmly. The jefe looks uncertain but he lets it go,

"Kemena." He says and a beautiful lady wearing a similar headdress but with flowers steps forward.

"This is my wife. Kemena, she is the Jefa." The jefe says as Kemena stands beside him, one hand on

His shoulder, a long knife in her other. She smiled at me. A warning smile. I smiled back. The Jefe

Turned his head and whispered something to Kemena, she nodded and walked away. "Have you met

Antonio?" the Jefe asked me, gesturing to Antonio. "Yes." I nodded. Kemena came back, holding the

Hand of a young boy, and behind her came a girl who looked older than me. Jefe Yatzil stood up he

Walked toward me. "This is my daughter, Salvadora Yatzil. Next year, she is going to be old enough

To be the new leader of our tribe." The chief looked proudly at his daughter, and Salvadora puffed

Up her chest and smiled. "Salvadora, get the necklaces please." Kemena told her daughter.

Salvadora threw her spear at the young boy, he caught it, and Salvadora bolted away. "What

Necklaces?" I asked the jefe, turning to him. "Ah, these necklaces are so that no other tribe will

Harm you. So that, they know that we have claimed ownership of you." He said, I raised my

Eyebrows. Claimed ownership? I don't like how that sounds. Salvadora handed 3 necklaces to

The Jefe. He tied a green necklace around my neck. It glistened in the sunlight, although it was

Nothing fancy. Just a green stone. He tied the red one around my dad's neck, and a yellow one

Around Bronwyn's neck. All the tribe members started howling. Instinctively, I stepped toward

Bronwyn. "It's alright," Antonio whispered, "It's just a celebration."

5

Catch the Crazy Tribal Kid

4 days later, I was sprinting through the wood, playing a game of 'catch the crazy tribal kid'.

Bronwyn was laughing and giggling as I tied him to my back the way the tribe people do. It was

Dangerous for me to be in this situation. In the woods, with crazy people. But they seemed nice.

And I already felt like I knew the woods like the back of my hand. Totonac, Antonio's 7 year old

Brother dashed through the woods and I saw a glimpse of his wild hair, and I grabbed his shirt.

Both of us ran, with me still holding on. And I tripped over a tree root. Falling hard to the forest

Floor. My head was spinning. Totonac whizzed away, not turning around. I slowly got up rubbing

My head. "Ot?" Bronwyn asked me. "Yeah?" I answered. "Where, we?" he asked, "I want, camp."

He said squirming around on my back. "Yeah, Bron, I'm tryna figure that out." Someone

Whizzed behind us, and I turned. Then the other direction, and I turned again. A drop of water fell

On my nose as I looked up. I saw a pair of eyes, they disappeared as quick as they came.

There was rustling in the branches behind me. Don't move. Don't breath. Don't-

I turned around quick as whoever it was tapped my shoulder, I held out my fists to their face,

My eyes still closed. That someone grabbed my fist and lowered it. I slowly opened one eye,

Then another. And I breathed a sigh of relief as the person I saw before me was none other

Than Salvadora, with an amused and quizzical look on her face. "Oh, Salvadora, you have no idea

How scared I was!" I exclaimed. She raised her eyebrows, "Yeah... I think I do." Then she beckoned

To me, "C'mon." "Salvadora," I started frowning, "I saw... I saw a pair of eyes... and they just...

Disappeared. I think I,- nothing." Salvadora whirled around, she gave me a nervous little chuckle

"Eyes?" she gave a little laugh, "Oh, oh, you got scared because of the owls. You know? Very

Common in this area." She said matter of factly and continued walking. "Owls are nocturnal

Animals..." I muttered to myself. "We're here!" Salvadora announced, bolting off, her arms in

The air. "Aaawoooo!" she howled, and disappeared. Whew. At least we were back in camp.

"Da-da." Bronwyn squirmed on my back, so I took of the rope and lowered him to the ground.

He waddled off in a direction where my dad was coming from. "Da-da!" he said lifting his arms.

"Hello Bronze, hello Otter. Where have you guys been?" he asked me picking up Bronwyn.

"Woo-d." Bronwyn said. "Oh really?" dad asked. Bronwyn started squirming so dad put him down,

And he ran-waddled off to play with the other littles. Dad and the Jefe went inside a tent and a

Boy, about a little older than my age came out. He tossed his dark, wavy hair, and looked at me.

He had hazel brown eyes. He came closer, and he smiled. I smiled back, uncertainly.

"Hey," he said, "My names Mateo." He introduced himself. "I'm Au-" I started, "Yvette Whitlock."

I announced. "Well, Yvette. I wanted to let you know," he said, his hands behind his back. "there's a

campfire tonight, if you wanna come?" he said, "Yes, I will be there." I said, he grinned, and ran away.

Later that night during the campfire, I saw Mateo again. I waved back as he waved to me and continued

singing their tribal song. I joined in too. Later that night, me, Mateo, Salvadora, Antonio, and a couple

other of the friends I made sat around a small campfire near a spring. "What does your name mean,

Yvette?" Micah, a boy around my age, with hair tied in a ponytail, asked me, poking the campfire. My

blood ran cold as I confidently lied "My name means the season of fall." "Hey!" Mateo exclaimed as if he

just woke up, "that's a season!" he exclaimed as if it was a great discovery. Everyone laughed.

I laughed too. "You're lucky that your names weird but unique. My name is just... weird." Antonio

Said. I looked at him, "Antonio, your name is the least weird name among everyone here. Even my

Name is weirder than yours." Everyone stared at me blankly. "Have you guys every been anywhere

Other than the wood?" I asked them, everyone shook their head. "In the outside world, your

Names are weird, my name is weird, even. But Antonio? That's the most common name among all

Of us." The rest of the night was spent in talking about, fizzy drinks, chips, and TV's.

6

A Suspect and a Case Uncovered

It was late in the afternoon, and out of the corner of my eye, I saw Antonio sneaking off somewhere.

I noticed this before, this was it, the suspense was killing me. So, I followed him, I know, I know, it's

Wrong. Everyone deserves one secret, but I'm sure he has other secrets too. Right? I saw the eyes

Again, following us, an occasional rustle behind me in the trees, that I know wasn't made by an

Animal. I saw a foot, even. Someone was following us, watching us. I thought I lost Antonio for a

Second. But I saw his bob of wild orange hair through the trees and ran to catch up, I hid behind a

Tree to watch him. He turned around, looked to see if anyone was there, and went on to a shed.

The sunlight hit it in an amazing angle and I gasped in awe, it was an old abandoned shed. But its

Magneticity still remained. With the sunlight pouring through the leaves of the trees it illuminated

Shed with green and yellow light. I crept closer and the door creaked open and Antonio stepped in

Cautiously, and shut the door behind him. I ran closer to the shed and tried to peer through the

Windows, but it was murky and I saw nothing. So, taking a deep breath and running through all the

Questions I wanted to ask him, I pushed open the door. Antonio spun around, blocking something

That was glowing with bioluminescent halo of blue. Weirder still, he was wearing a white lab coat.

"An-tonio?" I said breaking the word into 2 syllables. "Oh uh, Yvette. Didn't see you there." Nope, he

Definitely saw me there, I crossed my arms over my torso and raised my eyebrows. Antonio sighed

And moved aside revealing an old laptop. It was whirring buzzing and clicking. Like a zombie to a

Bowl of brains, I walked hypnotized toward the laptop, my fingers hovering over the keys. I stood up

Straight, and looked Antonio sharply in the eyes. "What are you doing here? What is this place?

Where did you get this laptop from? Why are you hiding-" I said, with a tone of anger. Antonio held

His hands out in front him, he looked vaguely alarmed. "Yvette, I never meant too. I just love

Science and my experiments. And about the laptop, The Jefe, the chief," he said taking a step closer,

"Would take it away, destroy it probably." He looked sorry and guilty, so I dropped my hands to my

Sides and sighed, nodding. "I get it. Now I gotta tell you something too." I told him about the eyes,

Leg, how his sister was acting weird when I mentioned it, and then, "I won't tell anyone is you

Won't." I concluded satisfied. He nodded and sat down on a spinny chair. "Yeah I noticed these

Things too. And I have bunch of questions as well. Why is my hair orange and not brown like

Everyone else's?" he said, waiting for an answer. I didn't want to venture there, I didn't want to

Upset Antonio, really, but I said it anyways. "Maybe... Maybe you were adopted?" I grimaced,

But he just nodded, he said, "Jefe said he and Mama found me in the woods, my parents,

Abandoned me..." he said sadly. I shook my head, "I'm sure there was a reason." I said comfortingly.

"I want to find out the truth," said Antonio downtrodden, "and I'm sure, I'm sure that its in here

Somewhere. This is the only inaccessible thing in here, its locked." He said pounding on a frayed

Cupboard, "Mhm." I nodded, I didn't even have to put effort, the cupboard was leg level, and I

Just reached down and pulled, but it remained closed. "Okay, I think I'd better go." I said as Antonio

Nodded, I slipped on something and to regain my balance I grabbed a counter kind of thing and

My leg hit the locked cupboard and it creaked open, I stopped midway, staring at it, and slowly

Lowered my leg. None of us moved. A gust of wind blew in through a crack and the cupboard

Creaked menacingly, Antonio jumped as if he were in a daze and jerked the handle back. The

Smell was dank, musty, and ancient. "I-" I started, "This, this is the truth, Yvette!" he exclaimed a

Wild look in his eyes. "Hold that torch here." He instructed, he squatted down and rummaged

For a while coughing multiple times in the process, and then he drew in a sharp breath and

Slowly pulled out an orange file. He blew on it and the dust flew off, the both of us sat on the

Floor looking at the file, it said "MARTINEZ CASE" in bold black letters.

I suddenly lurched for it scaring Antonio and flipped open to the first page. It read,

'On 2003, November 8th. Bissi Martinez wife of Nico Martinez was shot and killed along with her husband. The culprits of this case are the Los Zetas tribe. Bissi was shot near the nape of her neck.'

Saying that an image of Bissi lying in the grass with a blood coming out of her neck, and a mans

Arm in the background behind her, and a brown boot on the other side.

'Nico Martinez was shot in the same place Bissi was shot. The only living person in this crime scene is their son. Antonio Martinez.' Those two words echoed around the silent cabin. "There has to be some kind of mistake."

Antonio said, flipping to the next page. But what he found was even worse.

A picture of Bissi with a smiling baby in her arms. Antonio. He leaned back, dazed. And I flipped to

The next page. 'The only remaining family of Antonio Martinez is Euria Winchester, sister of Bissi.'

I choked, sister? Mum never mentioned that we had an aunt. Me and Antonio stared at each other.

"That means... we're cousins. Biologically." I said, a flicker of hope. Antonio nodded, then he stood

Up. Shoving the file under his arm, I stood up too. "I'm going to confront the Jefe. And, the Jefa." He

Said looking away, I could feel it, his heart weighed 100 tons. Each word breaking it, piece by piece.

He turned away, "Wait, Antonio." I said, laying a hand on his shoulder. "don't think I didn't notice

How you said Jefa instead of Mama. Wait, let's play it cool, we don't know who wrote this, and

who's in on this. I think we should tell my dad, only. And not tell anyone about the shed."

"Alright," he said solemnly, hiding the file.

We walked back to the wood in silence, "So," I said turning to Antonio. "I'm sorry about,

Everything." I said vividly gesturing in the air. "Its not your fault." He said and went off. I felt

Really bad for him, and I wished I could help.

Wait, I could help.

7

A Bit of Information

I stood in front of Dad, a minute later panting. "Dad," I gasped, hunching over, out of breath. "I

Need to talk to you. Privately." I gulped. Dad nodded and he led me to a clearing. "Who is

Euria?" I asked him, he looked shocked. "Autumn," he said mindful to keep his voice down.

"She is your mother." I nodded, "Who is Bissi Martinez?" Dad looked up slowly and cleared his

Throat. "Autumn I-" "Who, is, Bissi, Martinez?" I insisted. "She, she's your Mother's sister, hon."

He said, "Tell me about her dad, please." I said taking his hand, he sighed, his expression

Softened "I've only met her once or twice. She's a wild spirit that one, thinks after she talks.

Very carefree person. Married some guy called, Nico, I reckon. Never met him. And they had a son.

That's all I know, Otter." I nodded, "Thank you, dad."

8

The Confrontation?

I walked quickly, smiling nervously at everyone as I reached Antonio. He was sitting on a tree stump, lost

in thought, poking at the ground with a stick. "Antonio," I hissed. "Hmm?" he said looking up. "I

confirmed it with my Dad. I'm sorry..." I mumbled, he stood up, stepping on the stick. "Let's go." he

muttered angrily. "Where?" I asked tagging behind him uselessly. "To confront the Jefa and Jefe." he

said his jaw set, "Antonio, please wait," I said pulling him back. "We need to know proper, solid facts."

I pleaded. "Until then, just ask him subtle questions about your parents," I said. He nodded grimly and

darted inside the Jefe's tent.

"Jefe Yatzil," he said bowing down in front of the chief. I couldn't see, or hear clearly, but this was

enough. "What is it?" the chief said impatiently. "I, I found two weird-looking names in the information

tent. The names were Nico and Bissi I think." He said pronouncing them weirdly. The Jefe leaned forward

nodding. "Can you tell me more about them?" he asked tentatively keeping his eyes glued to the floor.

The Jefe nodded. "Oh, some stupid scientist foreigners. The woman was a real mad one though." the Jefe

dismissed with wild hand gestures. I cringed inwardly, "Thank you," Antonio said through gritted teeth.

and left.

9

The Confrontation.

"I'm sorry about that, I shouldn't have insisted-" I said, "No," Antonio replied. "Thank you. Now I know

that they are the ones who killed my parents," he said. "The Los Zetas is the most dangerous tribe in

Mexico, I think we should leave." I said looking up at him, "Where would we go?" he asked, "Anywhere but

here." I said. "That's it, I'm confronting them, I've had enough of living in the dark." he stood up.

I should have stopped him,

It would be the right thing to do.

But...

I've stopped him enough.

But a lingering thought stopped me from not stopping him...

"Antonio, wait!" I said jogging to catch up with him. "Think this through, Antonio, please. I know this is

a lot to process. Antonio... I have a plan." I nagged at him until he finally turned around, "What is it?"

he said impatiently with a mad glint in his eyes.

I did *not* have a plan.

"Can you wait till midnight?" I asked him, tentatively. "We can steal the gun which your dad- I'm sorry, I mean, the Jefe used to shoot your parents. We'll have something to defend ourselves with. You know how dangerous they can be... So please don't make stupid decisions." "I know where the gun is." he said gruffly, I nodded.

Under the moonlight, two figures crept across a silent camp, where the flames from a fire flickered to resemble their hopes. The figures stopped in front of a tent, their dark silhouettes reflecting on the ancient white fabric.

Antonio slowly crept in. His dad snoring away on the cot. Antonio kneeled down on the cold floor, and he pulled out a black brief-case, he opened the latch softly and pulled out a black gun. The Jefe gave loud snore startling Antonio and he banged his head to a lamp.

The Jefe woke up, his bloodshot eyes looking wounded and scarred in the candlelight. Antonio darted under the bed, "Wah - What, who's there?" The Jefe slurred, Antonio, holding his breath. The Jefe crashed back onto the cot. With the swiftness of a monkey (monkeys are *not* swift.) Antonio dove out of the tent. Taking a gasp of fresh air. He brandished the gun in the air proudly. "You did it!" I squealed breathlessly.

There is never a happy ending for people like you and me.

The Jefe staggered onto the plain. "Antonio, Antonio, Antonio..." he slurred, "I am your Dad! I. AM. THE. JEFE!" he roared, swaggering closer and closer to us. The Jefa creeped out behind him, looking between us and him frantically with wide eyes. She rushed forward putting her thin hand on the Jefe's shoulder.

"Querido, calm down." she purred, he shrugged of her shoulder. "Mi amor, please." she said, tugging him back. With one final roar, he pushed her off and she fell to the forest ground.

One gunshot.

The Jefe fell to the floor, he roared and staggered up, blood seeping from his arm. "Don't touch her!!" Antonio yelled holding the smoking gun. The Jefa hit Cheif Yatzil on the head with a branch, and he crumpled to the ground in an useless heap. "Mi niño. Mi amor. Mi querido. I'm sorry, please, go!! I love you." Jefa Yatzil said. Antonio froze in his spot then dropped the gun on the floor and dashed to the Jefa. "I'm sorry Mama," he said, embracing her for the last time, she brushed his cheek and planted a kiss on his forehead. "Go," she said, her eyes fluttering close. I rushed to our tent and woke Dad up.

"Dad, Dad!!!" I hissed. "Wuh - What?" he bolted up, "We have to go!" I said pulling him up. "Where?" he said dragging a hand across his face. "Antonio shot the Jefe because he found out the Jefe killed his parents. His parents are Bissi and Nico Martinez by the way. Now come on!" I rushed.

Which ever part Dad comprehended he was on his feet and strapping Bronwyn to his back, we rushed back out to see several lights turning on in several tents and many shouts. I dragged Dad and Antonio away into the forest.

10

A New Beginning...

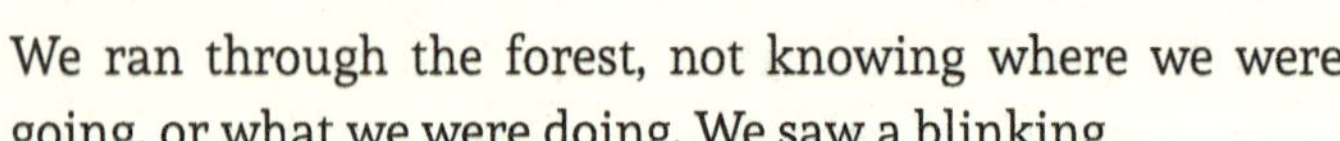

We ran through the forest, not knowing where we were going, or what we were doing. We saw a blinking light in the far distance, and a dirt road. We reached a ship port after 2 hours, all of us wet, dirty, tired, and miserable. The rain persisted, threatening to strike with lightning any second we stepped out of our coven.

The rain battering against the shattered tiles.

Testing our will.

We didn't push through.

We just fell asleep.

. . .

"Oi!" a voice shouted. "Oi! Hey! who's over there?" a man came over. Through blinking eyes I watched Dad get up and shake hands with a man who was wearing a raincoat and had a weird mustache. "Ah..." I heard the man say, scratching his chin and squinting. Dad and the man went off into the distance to talk. I closed my eyes. Dad shook me awake. "Otter? Otter?" he said, softly shaking my shoulder. "My buddy, Jose here hooked us on a ship to the UK. I have a friend there too, who can, uh, figure something out for us." He said, all the while not looking into my eyes. I sat up, "Dad, whats wrong?" I said. I saw it. He quickly

glanced at his hand, which... Didn't have a ring on it. I gasped in shock, "Dad! Your ring-" "Take your

things we're leaving now." he said, his jaw set with determination.

But past it all, I willed him to look into my eyes, and I saw a vulnerable, hurt man.

Dad ruffled my hair and pulled me up. "My silver, my silver most precious than gold.?" he sang holding

my hand and waltzing me around. "In the moonlight how you shine, I shall watch you shine?" he

croaked. I don't know how he was doing this, it was Mum's favorite song."Come on!!" he said, twirling and

turning. "My silver, my silver most precious than gold. In the moonlight how you shine, I shall watch you

glow. ?" I sang, sobbed, and laughed. "We can do this." he said looking directly into my eyes, clasping

both my hands together. I nodded.

We could.

We can do this.

And we will do this.

11

S. S. The Old Avocado.

Yes, our ship's name is S.S. The Old Avocado. Or El Viejo Aguacate. Everyone just calls the ship Old Eva.

The day dragged on in a dreary blur and all we saw was water for miles to come. The only ’shocking‘ event was that a celebrity decided to grace us with his presence. It was hard to size him up but I can try, he was a fat, rich man, with a narcissistic air of self-importance around him. To his arm clung a glamourous lady with dark purple hair, a leopard print gown, with a white fur coat, and sunglasses. They were followed by an entourage of nervous, try-hard attendees. Jose gave us an empty cabin and promised us food. He finally walked upto us at dusk and showed us our cabin which had 3 rickety beds.

That night's sleep wasn't peaceful.

Why was everything cold? And wet? And... Dark?? A sudden surge of water hit my face explosively. I tried to breathe but I couldn't, I couldn't find air. I couldn't find land. I tried to pull myself up and only sank deeper. The water had a proper grip on my feet pulling me down into the murky abyss below. I gave one final push and came up. With a desperate gasp for air, I collapsed onto land and limped further, and further and I saw a light. I scrambled closer to it and saw... Mom. A ghostly figure of her glowing. She smiled down at me and floated toward me. "My child..." the wind carried her angelic voice and every word sounded like a melody, dancing in my ears. How I had longed to hear that voice again... "Mom?" I asked reaching out to touch her. "I'm so sorry," she said enveloping me in a hug. I breathed in her jasmine scent, tears welling in my eyes. "I love you," she said stroking my cheek, with a pained expression. I grasped at her hand and her cold fingers brushed mine longingly as she faded away. The water rose, it crashed over me. I woke up, I was astonished to find myself gripping the cold bedpost of the rickety bed. I sat up on one elbow and gazed outside. Endless blues, the sun rose slowly as mist slowly cleared from the window. I stretched and just as my feet touched the cold floor, a shrill shriek echoed through the whole ship. Another shriek, and then a blood-curdling and ghostly sob. Dad woke up, sat up and frowned at me, I shrugged back at him. I woke Antonio up and he sleepily lumbered off the bed and scratched his head. We headed outside to see a mass of scared people holding lamps and torches and whispering between themselves. "Help!!" the same voice cried from earlier and we all surged in a different direction. The whispering grew louder and louder until someone yelled, "I'm gonna get the captain!" and there were several murmurs of approval. We pushed further and further through the crowd and saw the rich man from earlier. He lay dead on the ground, I was taken aback, my eyes widened in surprise. Where were his loyal staff and attendees now that their master was dead? The same purple-haired lady was wearing a black satin nightgown and was kneeling down on the carpet, and an orange-haired lady wearing a white silk nightgown lay crouched beside her. "Serphina, darling, calm down." she purred, her perfectly manicured hand on Serphina's shoulder. "But Octavia!" Serphina burst out, "Someone killed him, and that someone is on this ship!" she wailed. "Yes, hunny, you're right." Octavia nodded anxiously. The Captain came running, sweating profusely. "What seems to be the prob-" he said as he followed everyone's eyes to the dead body, the Captain yelped, clutching his cap to his chest in horror. "No!" he yelped, "Its our ships richest, most important guest, who is also our brand ambassador!!" he said falling to the floor in a kneeling position in a defeated way. "Everyone back to your cabins," he said his eyes still fixed on the man, he waved his cap lazily at everyone, and the crowd began to disperse. A redhead crew boy with freckles came running up, and surveyed the scene in horror. "Captain?" he stuttered, tears welling in his eyes, he wasn't that old, 13-14 years old at most. And he looked sensitive. "Come now, Kai." the Captain said getting up.

"Is it really that much of a big deal, Captain?" Kai whimpered, the Captain stopped walking and put a hand on Kai's shoulder and said, "Boy, this is the most important passenger we have. And he's dead." he said, pursing his lips. "Whats his name?" Kai asked, "Montgomery Vanderbelt." the Captain said with vivid gestures. "Now run along, Kai." the Captain said patting his back, Kai ran off. The Captain turned to us.

We were the only ones remaining there other than Octavia and Serphina. The Captain marched toward

us. "Names Pierre. Do we... uh, have a problem?" he asked squinting, hands on his hips. "None at all sir."

Dad said and dragged us away. I told Dad I'd spy on them because I had a suspicion, and surprisingly, he

agreed. The Captain's back was turned, so me and Antonio darted inside a broom closet and we could see

and hear everything clearly. "I'm sorry for your loss ma'am." the Captain said, and he left. Serphina's

tearful expression changed to an annoyed one. "Ugh," she said, "His skin was so thick, it was impossible

for him to die if I stabbed him just once." she drawled, checking her nails. "Girlll... Forget that, acting was

so hard. I was almost gonna laugh!" Octavia said. "Yeah, but at least crying wasn't." Serphina grinned and

dropped a vial of glycerin on the carpet, it clinked dully and landed near Octavia's foot, and she kicked it

away, the pair gleefully laughed. "I think I broke a nail!" Octavia whined, "Let's go," Serphina gave one

disgusted look at Montgomery and lightly nudged him with her foot. "Yup, he's dead," she confirmed and

they both giggled again and sashayed their way into their cabin. All this while, I had my eyes only on one

thing. The *innocent* bottle of glycerin on the carpet, I took in a sharp breath before going for the bottle

and bursting out of the closet. I held the bottle by its moist wrapper which was unraveling at this point.

Without the explanation I owed Antonio, I raced back to our cabin, where Dad was waiting patiently, gazing out of the window. "Dad," I gulped, motioning to Antonio to lock the door. "I've got proof," I said proudly and produced the bottle of glycerin. "This is the bottle of glycerin that Serphina and Octavia used to make Serphina cry," I said slowly taking off the wrapper and wrapping the bottle in a plastic cover which was lodged behind the cupboard. "This will have their fingerprints on it, and we can show it to the police." I said triumphantly shoving the cover into one of the cupboard drawers. "But what were they after?" Antonio asked, "Montgomery's money." Dad snarled. I nodded, "It's a terrible thing to do, kill someone for their money." Dad spat. Antonio's eyes widened, "They do that?"

It was kinda silly, really, Antonio was like an innocent little kid, forever asking questions. But in reality, He's more adult than most of us.

I smile softly at him, and he furrows his eyebrows still and looks at Dad. "Yeah bud," Dad says, "they do that." Antonio grapples with that thought for a second, "I'm sorry sir," he says briefly, "I'm not very familiar with everything in the, y'know, outside world." he says fidgeting with his hands nervously.

Dad places a firm hand on Antonio's shoulder and Antonio's eyes open wide in fear, "You can call me Uncle Adam or just Adam, if you like." Dad says softly, Antonio is taken aback and moved, no one has said such a kind thing to him before, I can see it. The familiar look of confusion crosses over his face, "Isn't your name, Gatsby?" he asks, dad scratches the back of his head, "About that..." he begins to say but I quickly cut him off, we have to tread lightly with this one. "We didn't exactly trust the Jefe, I had read about the Los Zetas tribe in my school textbook, and I knew something was off, so I... told them fake

names just in case. And Antonio? When just you, me, Dad, and Bronwyn are around, you can call me

Autumn, Dad Uncle Adam, and Bronwyn, Bronwyn. But when we're in public, I think it's better for you to

call me Yvette, Dad Gatsby, and Bronwyn Atlas. And your undercover name is..." I thought for a second,

"Liam Hawksworth," I said finally, Antonio nodded with a pleased expression on his face. "Alright guys,

let's get to sleep, we have a big day tomorrow." Dad said clapping his hands, plonking Bronwyn onto the

bed. Bronwyn's bottom lip quivered, his eyes glassy with tears and he began to whine. Dad sat down on

the bed next to him. He placed a hand on Bronwyn's back, with his hand taking up most of his back, Dad

pulled him closer slowly a knowing look in his eyes, a grimace, because... Because Dad knew what was

coming and I did too. I sighed, tears welling in my eyes too, I sniffled and tried to stay strong. "Hey, what's

wrong buddy?" Dad asked even though he already knew the answer, Bronwyn sniveled like a whimpering

puppy. "Mama!" he said. Dad sighed, I joined them on the bed. "I, Mama." he sniffled sadly. "You can... go

to Mama later Bron." Dad huffed tiredly, "No." I said placing a hand on Dad's hand. I turned to Bronwyn

and took his tiny hand in mine. "Bronwyn, Mama is... Not coming back." I said, swiping aggressively at my

eyes, "Where, Mama?" asks Bronwyn, "Mama is gone, Bronwyn." I say gently. What processed in

Bronwyn's mind was not what I expected to be processed. He nodded his little head in a wise manner, as if he understood everything, he lay down, pulled the blanket over himself and nodded saying, "Ok,

I see, Mama, tomorrow." and then he closed his eyes, his tiny fists tightly curled around the blanket. I

kissed his forehead softly as he squinted his eyes. I flicked off the lights and climbed into bed. Only 4

nights left for us to go to London. And then... A new beginning, I guess. One far, far away from home.

After all, how could I go home if I didn't know where home was? I sighed, and without expecting it,

closed my eyes and drifted into a dreamless sleep. At least that's what I thought and what I hoped for...

And I was under the water again, I dove up and I saw ice. Cold, threatening ice creeping toward me

slowly. The water and ice froze me waist down and I shrieked because it felt like a thousand needles

were piercing me. I thumped on the ice and screamed my lungs out, as dark silhouettes crossed under

the ice, brushing my legs. One ghostly white figure pressed its face against the surface. First, wild strands

of matted, orange hair. Then a creased forehead and then dull brown eyes with sagging dark circles and

bags under them. A nose, and a cracked, dry mouth. The whole face was pale and wore a solemn

expression. "Mom?" I asked, thumping on the ice, harder, "Mom, Mom!!" I searched the face for any signs

of life, anything at all. But there were none... The ice cracked suddenly and hands dragged me under the

water and that was it. I was up and shaking. I was shivering as if the temperature was below -1 degrees. It

took me a few minutes to process the shock thoroughly. And once I did, I stood up and walked right ' outside the door and out onto the deck. I paced slowly at first and I walked faster, and faster as my thoughts flew by until I broke into a run. I get it. I get what I had done wrong. What I was doing wrong.

I wasn't giving myself enough time to process the thought. The idea that she really died, and as I stood on the deck, leaning over the rail, the moonlight casting its comforting glow over me. I couldn't believe it.

"Is Mom really dead?" I asked myself sadly. "Yeah," I say uncertainly, because, I'm not sure. See, I'm not sure if my mom died or not because I never had time to process anything else. I should have been okay with this really, because my whole life no one has ever given me time to process or adjust to anything.

But right now is the time I should give myself. I sat on an abandoned deck chair, which creaked with anticipation carrying all my sudden emotions. As I sat on that abandoned deck chair, its weathered wood groaning beneath me, I felt a tidal wave of emotions crashing over me. Tears streamed down my cheeks, unchecked and unstoppable, as the weight of my loss bore down on me like a heavy stone. Each sob wracked my body, echoing the ache in my heart. My chest tightened with grief, a relentless ache that seemed to have no end. The absence of her laughter, her warmth, her love, felt like a gaping chasm in my life, one that threatened to swallow me whole. I clutched at the fabric of my shirt, fingers trembling as I tried to hold myself together. But the grief was relentless, overwhelming, consuming me from the inside out. Memories of her flooded my mind, each one a bittersweet reminder of what I had lost. The breeze whispered around me, a gentle caress against my skin that offered no solace. The world around me seemed to blur, the colors muted by the tears that filled my eyes. In that moment, I felt utterly alone. Lost in a sea of sorrow, adrift without her guiding light to lead me home. And as the moon dissapeared behind the clouds, I let out a keening cry, a sound of anguish that echoed through the empty space around me.

For in that moment, I realized that she was truly gone. And no amount of tears could ever bring her back.

I stumbled off the chair and into my cabin, dragging a sweaty hand across my face, and collapsed into bed.

The next morning to my shock, I woke to a soaked pillow and a hole in my shirt. I grumbled as I slipped off the bed. I staggered into the bathroom and peered at my weary face in the mirror. A little bit of redness remained on my face and I splashed it with water, other than that my shirt was wrinkled and creased and had a sizable hole in it. I poked my finger through it and "Ugh." The damage done was unrepairable.

Whatever, I shrugged it off and put on the same clothes again. They were beginning to smell of mud, leaves, rain, and sweat. And just as I was stepping out of the washroom Dad woke up, and I asked, "What was the big day we have planned today?" I ask as the sun slowly rises over the horizon and casts its pale orange and pink glow all through the room, pure and unfiltered. It pours into every corner of the room and trys to find a way into Antonio's sealed eyes until he gives up and wakes up, rubbing his eyes and stretching his arms. "It's sunny." He croaks, "Listen up guys." Dad says seriously, squinting in the light.

"We're gonna borrow some clothes from the souvenir store today," Dad says. I laugh, and Dad looks at me gravely, my mouth forms a single O. "You can't be serious?" I say.

Dad was serious. And we are nervously striding toward the souvenir store. And Antonio is to distract the cashier. We walk into the air-conditioned room, and immediately I know this store sells *everything.* I see air-dried candies, wigs, electronic fans, guitar strings, slime, indoor plants, laces and literally so many more of the most random things. I just stare in shock. Bronwyn lets go of Dad's hand and waddles off in a hurry to examine the colorful contents of the store with Dad after him. Antonio stumbles toward the counter where there stands a boy who looks around 19 to 20 with ratty brown hair, acne, glasses and a green cardigan with a name badge with the fading name 'Gregory' written on it. Silently revising what we told him to say in his head and also mouthing the words. "Hello, sir." he says in a very automated voice as he shuffles closer toward the counter. Gregory looks up suspiciously and raises an eyebrow skeptically.

"How may I help?" he says, "I need a..." Antonio says searching his head "Mango." I hold my head in my hands. Great. A mango. Gregory steps out from behind the counter and disappears for barely a second and comes back with a fresh, yellow mango, and he dumps it in Antonio's hands with a smug smile. "Anything else I can do for you sir?" he asks briskly, "I don't want the mango." Antonio says. "Wha- Why?" Gregory asks, "I'm allergic." Antonio makes choking noises and moves closer to Gregory as Gregory backs further away. "Then why'd you ask for it?" he snaps. "I-" Antonio says and collapses on the floor hurling the mango at Gregory missing his hair by an inch. Gregory yelps and hurries down the corridor yelling "Mangos!! Captain!" with his arms flailing wildly in the air behind him. We immediately grab suitcases and begin loading them with clothes and snacks and whatnot. The clothes are either a bit too big or a bit to small, but at least we finally have fresh pairs of clothes. We quickly brisk-walk back to our cabin and I change my clothes. It feels good to finally be in a pair of clean clothes. Feeling refreshed, I think that it was finally the right time to have a talk with Dad. "Antonio, do you mind watching Bronwyn for a couple of minutes?" I ask him and he nods, taking Bronwyn by the hand and taking out a couple of toys from the suitcase. Me and Dad step out and walk to the deck, Dad has no clue what this is about. And I'm glad, because he needs a fresh perspective. "Whats wrong, sweetheart?" He asks worriedly. I point him to the same deck chair as last night and sit down in an opposite one and lean forward with my clasped hands resting on my knees. "Dad," I say gently and reach out to take his hand, "Mom is dead." this hits him the same way it hits me, a flash of something vague crosses his face, and he turns his head. "Enough of this." I say sternly. "My whole life," I say in a pained tone, "We were moving place to place. And no one ever asked me how I felt about it, and I didn't really care either. I loved the adventure of it, because you and Mom were always there if I had a problem. But Mom is gone, and look Dad, I'm used to adjusting to everything, and don't get me wrong. I like it. It just... Goes by quickly and I like to look at the good side of things. But, you and I... We haven't given ourselves time to process the fact that Mom is really gone."

I search his face, he turns to look at me. I give him a big hug and disappear back to the cabin. I try to have a bright and everything-is-fine expression. "Only 3 more days until we're in London." I chirped.

"London?" Antonio asks, "Its the place we're going to." I reply, "Is it anything like back at home?" Antonio questions. He may not miss his 'parents.' But he definitely misses his home. I would too if I lived there my whole life. The woods full of life, the variety of trees, the fresh, cool, clear streams. I miss it already.

"Not at all." I reply, "I've been to London before. I made a friend there, her name was Agatha Stone. She was really nice and naive. She had brain cancer and no one would be her friend. But we got along well together. She was petite and fragile. But had a really lively spirit nonetheless. She had a trauma from her childhood that had left her scarred. Her Dad was always working and never made enough time for her and her sister. So was her Mom. Her Dad's job needed her Dad to go on business trips abroad and they didn't see him often. They had big debts which were made by Agatha's paternal grandfather. And her mother worked part-time jobs. Once, when Agatha was 7 and her sister was 10. As usual her Dad was on a business trip and her Mom was at work. So the sisters were home alone. A man crept into the house and Agatha and her sister, Agnes heard it and ran upstairs and locked the door. Agnes pushed Agatha into a closet and shut the door just as the man barged into the room and demanded where the valuables where

kept. Poor Agnes didn't know and the man shot her in the head and left. Agatha crept out of the closet

and called her Mom from an old barely functioning telephone and told her everything that had happened.

Agatha's father rushed home from Belgium the next day and a month later the family found out that

Agatha had brain cancer. The loss of Agnes hit Agatha the hardest because Agnes was like a mother to

her. And I remember Agatha's heartbroken expression when I told her I was leaving. She said I reminded

her of Agnes..." A tear escaped my eye, and I quickly wiped it away. Antonio stood rigidly. I get it, he

doesn't know what to do, never been in this situation before. "Its fine, you don't have to say anything." I

reassure him just as Dad walks in with his face looking red, puffy, and blotched. I was glad he cried it out.

I glimpse at his face, he briefly smiles at me. That smile means thank you. I nod my head back. Good.

The day passes on regularly and except for me occasionally checking on the 'proof' we found. The night

went on blissfully with no nightmares. 2 days left for London. I thought when I woke up. I showered put

on clean clothes and went to breakfast to grab a waffle or two. After that, I was just walking in the ship

when I found out there was a pool. In the ship. I was ecstatic. I changed and immediately dove in. I loved

the blissful feel of the water all around me as I danced and dove around the pool. I practiced and practiced

until noon till I was starving. I ate everything in triple servings and drying my hair walked to our cabin.

No one. They must be strolling the deck too. It was the near to last day and I had only found out that this ship had so much stuff to do. I walked into a room and gaped. Utter chaos. Different colors of blinking lights, people yelling, loud music. And the biggest problem. Which arcade game should I play? All of them. I decided. It was probably 7 when I went back to our cabin and Jose brought us dinner. Soup and bread. Dinner was most crowded and Jose did his best to bring us whatever he could. Skip forward and... Cue the nightmares. I was locked in a dark space with another girl. I looked at her. Agatha. A younger version of her. She looked terrified as yellow light filtered through the slits in the door and cast a glow on her face. She glanced at me and back, her fingers tensing as she gripped the door. Another girl who looked vaguely similar to Agatha stood outside looking at the door. And a man dressed in complete black barged in holding a gun. "Where is all the money?" he growled. Agnes backed away terrified, "I, I, I don't-" she said but the man shot her, a clean shot through her head. I stifled a scream, and Agatha's mouth was wide open in a silent scream. Before dying Agnes turned her head toward the closet and smiled. The man circled the room and opened the closet door. Something grabbed me from behind and pulled me back, into its safety. Agatha's face aged, she grew taller, her hair longer. "Don't go," she said softly. I tried to open my mouth to tell her that I wanted to stay. "Don't go!!!" she screamed as the man shot her. I screamed. Then I realized nothing was pulling me back. I could have helped her. I could have. I could have saved her. I could have.

The man peeked into the closet, pointing the gun to my head. Where were those hands that were dragging me back now? Why is there no one exactly when I need them? I closed my hands over my ears, and slid down the wall slowly with my back pressed, bending my head. And the man shot me. "Agatha!!" I woke up screaming. "No, no, no." I muttered getting up and racing into the washroom splashing my face with cold water. I stare at my reflection. Ok, ok, everything is fine. I go back into the cabin and stare at my bed.

The blanket is in a heap on the floor. No. I can't sleep here. I grab my blanket and my pillow and drop my pillow in the bathtub and climb in, pulling the blanket tightly around me. I don't know how long it took me to finally fall asleep. But I did. And then I woke up and I blinked in the bright light and I heard muffled voices. Dad and Antonio stared down at me in confusion and amusement. I just yawned and stretched, acting as if this was completely normal behavior and gave them a hug. "Morning guys." I said. I picked up another pair of clean clothes and walked back into the washroom. A minute later I opened the bathroom and hurled my pillow and blanket out the door. Oops to who ever it hit. Sorry.

I took a bath and announced "1 day left!" To myself in the mirror. I changed into a pair of blue jeans and frilly white shirt. I dried my hair and stepped out. "You hit me with a pillow!" Antonio exclaimed indignantly, ohhh, so thats who it hit. I gave him an equally cross look for no reason, crossed my arms.

And then we both burst out laughing for no reason. I mean... I really don't know why!! After we were done, I went to get breakfast. An orange juice and french toast. Tomorrow was London. Tomorrow was a whole new beginning. I hope. I hope I can leave this life behind. I hope I can make friends. I hope I can forget about everything that happened. I hope we can settle in a place, any place. But I guess I can just keep hoping. Because I can hope alright. I can keep hoping, but when will those hopes come true?

Oh well. I shrug off that thought, and settle down at a corner table with a killer view. Fish jumped out of the water, their silver scales gleaming in the sunlight as they break the perfect blue water and dive back in. I felt content, I like this life. But I'm sure it wouldn't last forever. For someone like me, that's just pushing luck. I smile to myself at that thought, picturing myself in a sailors outfit, running around, sweeping the deck. I giggle escaped my mouth. Spending time with myself was helping me heal, I liked this atleast. I ate slowly, there was no hurry, was there? No there was none. Antonio came running just as I finished my second to last piece of toast and was downing my orange juice. "Autumn, you need to come. Now." He said, what could possibly be so important? I thought, still chugging my orange juice.

"Hurry up!!" he lowered his voice, "Its about, the proof." he hissed, I choked on my orange juice and immediately got up. I eyed the last piece of toast longingly and just grabbed it in my hand, made it a roll and shoved it in my mouth. The toast almost fell out my mouth when I saw the sight of our cabin. All the beds where pulled to the middle the mattresses leaning against the wall, the bed sheets, blankets, and pillows where all in a heap in the corner of the room. The 3 wardrobes had been opened and the hangers

lay on the floor, the drawers were pulled opened and our suitcases were ripped open, all our clothing

scattered in piles around it. My mouth hung open. Whoever did this, they were on to us. I turned in a slow

circle to survey the room, just as Dad came running and almost dropped Bronwyn. We got to work putting

the mattresses back on the bed frames, pulling on the bed sheets, and neatly folding the blanket. We put

our clothes were folded and kept back in the suitcase, the hangers back in their place in their wardrobe.

We moved the beds back to each corner of the room. Now was the final question, did they find it or not??

The three of us moved closer, and closer to the wardrobe which had the bottle of glycerin. In the process

of opening the drawer, the thief had jammed it. It took several minutes until we pulled the drawer open

and it was there alright, safe as ever in its plastic cover. I clutched it to my chest tightly and breathed a

half - sigh, half - gasp. "This can't stay here. It has to be far away from us." Dad said, I nodded. But... "Please

dad, let me keep it. I'll find a safe place for it I promise. Far away from us." I said. Dad raised his eyebrows,"

You sure otter? Because this is no child play, we're dealing with dangerous people." he said, a look of fear

crossed his eyes. "I'm sure Dad." I said, but where..?

I walked quickly to the arcade room. I darted and dodged the many kids and teenagers and went to the last

game I could find, and I stuffed it behind it. Satisfied with my work I dusted my hands. I caught a kid in a

black hoodie, with red eyes, glaring at me. I glared back until they looked away. Then I quietly slipped the whole cover into my jeans pocket and ran out of the arcade room. Dad said far away from us... I thought as guilt flooded my head. No. Everything would be just fine. "Where did you put it?" Antonio asked, "Secret."

I said playfully, "Some secret." Antonio muttered but caught me staring at him, and then we both just started laughing again. The four off us chilled on the deck until it was dinner and Jose brought us, bread, tomato soup, steamed vegetables, pasta, and icecream. Pasta and icecream!! "Thank you, thank you, Jose!"

I said, "Oh, yes, yes, yes, yes, yes, today is your last day after all." he said. I collapsed into bed and sent a silent prayer to god begging for no nightmares tonight. And there were no nightmares. Dad shook me awake with an urgent look on his face, "Yeah?" I asked sleepily. "Autumn, someone *destroyed* the arcade room." My blood ran ice cold, a tremor crawled up my spine. "Autumn... Where did you hide the proof?"

Dad hissed, "In the arcade room." I whispered. "Or so they thought." I replied with a somewhat smug and very relieved expression when I realized that the bottle was safe in my pocket. "Its in my pocket." I said softly. "Autumn." Dad grabs me by the shoulders, he looks mad. "You don't realize what you've done!" he roars. "I thought you were responsible, I thought I could trust you but no!" he says pacing around the room. My tears are falling fast now. "I, I'm sorry dad. I didn't want to put us in danger." I whisper. I must have looked really scared, terrified even. Because his expression turns soft in a matter of seconds and he rushes toward me, he hugs me and holds me tight and I cry into his shoulder. "My otter." he says caressing my cheek, "I am so sorry." he says wiping a tear, "You know how much I love you. I never meant to shout.

I just... Want to keep us safe. I couldn't, I couldn't keep mom safe you know?" he says his voice cracking,

and I know and I forgive Dad instantly. "I'm sorry Dad." I say, "No." he says kissing my forehead. "Get

ready, we're leaving in a hour, and give me the bottle of glycerin." I nod and hand him the cover. I glance

at him over the side of my eye and he's just staring at the cover. Antonio comes out of the washroom,

wearing, black jeans, and a grey t-shirt with a faded picture of a palm tree. We exchange a silent good-

morning through a nod and I step into the washroom. I undressed and a few minutes later, I'm standing

under a hot shower. It feels good, each drop of water clearing my thoughts. I wear a different pair of blue

jeans, with a black t -shirt, and blue hoodie. Tugging the hood over my head, I walked out of the

washroom. Dad nodded at me. Should I go to the arcade room? No, I don't even want to go in the direction

of that wretched place, I scowled at nothing in particular and headed in the direction of the arcade room

and found myself in the restaurant. It was vacant, except a family of 6, an old man and woman, and a man

in a business suit. I took my corner table, grabbed a couple of french toasts with a side of bacon and

strawberries. I pulled my hood lower over my face, but it was too late, the rich lady saw me. Serphina.

She narrowed her eyes, the strawberries got stuck in my throat. I coughed quietly, and Serphina points me

out to Octavia. I silently curse myself, its like I was *begging* to be noticed by them. I finished my last strip of greasy bacon, and savor the taste before running out of the restaurant. Yes. I'm sure of it. Those

witches are solely responsible for all the chaos. But their parade of joy is going to be over soon. I raced

back just in time and Dad and Antonio were lugging all our suitcases out with Bronwyn sitting on his and

Dad's suitcase, and giggling. A pinched his cheeks and patted his head. Then I whisked him away down the

hall saying 'Whoooosh!' as we went. My heart panged, and I stopped abruptly. Bronwyn is only 1 and-a-

half years old, what if he... Doesn't remember Mom? I choked back a sob, but it washed over me, and I

kneeled down on the carpeted floor and let the sobs shake me. I could hear Dad and Antonio abandon

their suitcases and come running. "Otter?" Dad panicked, "Autumn, whats wrong?" Antonio and Dad

sounded really worried. "Dad." I croaked, "What if Bronwyn forgets Mom?" I sniffled, "I, uh-" Dad

stuttered, Antonio placed a hand on Dad's shoulder, and an understanding passed through them. "Autumn,

uh, hey. Listen, I was taken from my parents when I was 7 months old. But I still have one memory which

I hold on to of my Mom and Dad. Me and Mom were sitting a grassy area on a blanket and she was holding

me, singing a lullaby. Dad came rushing and scooped me up, holding me in the air, they both laughed. I,

I've never met my parents, Autumn, but I miss them. I miss them so, so much." A pained look crosses his

face. "I've never seen a person as brave as you. I'd never share something like that. Thank you so much

Antonio, that made me feel a ton better." I said getting up, I meant every word of what I said. He blushes,

"Don't worry, Bronwyn will remember Aunt Euria," he says comfortingly, I nod. I trust that fact. Especially

because it came from him. And oh, he referred to Mom as Aunt Euria. I'm so lucky to have him as my

cousin among the 7 billion people in the world, I think silently. I just realized how nervous and excited I

am. I pull at the fabric of my shirt repeatedly.

12

Tea, Taxis, and Taxes.

We get of the ship and a light drizzle starts almost immediately. Jose hollers at Dad and Dad waves back.

"So... This is London?" Antonio says, yup. I survey the scene around me. The rain is picking up, traffic,

people in coats holding briefcases walking busily, a puff of smoke here and there. Ahh... London. "Yup." I

reply. Antonio is trying hard not to look dissapointed. Dad grabs my hand and with Bronwyn hoisted on

his shoulders the four of us cross the road. Antonio looks at the cars tenatively, "What're those?" he asks,

"Cars, we use them to go from one place to another, instead of walking." I say, we stand under a bus stop.

We are surrounded by a crowd of sorts. A short, portly, bald man in a top hat, puffing away busily at a

cigar, another man in a brown coat holding a pile of newspapers, an old woman wearing a grey raincoat,

and clutching a white purse, a little boy in overalls with his bicycle. Another plump

woman, with red hair, and black overcoat, holding an umbrella joins us under the bus stop. "These rains never stop." she huffs, Antonio's eyes widen. He's heard there accent for the first time. "Why do they talk like that?" he whispers to me looking genuinely astonished. "That's their accent." I hiss back, "They might think we talk funny." I say, just as the plump woman glances my way and I offer a brief smile, which she returns. After 5 to 10 minutes the rain stops and the whole crowd plus a few more people step out onto the pavement, "Where do we stay?" I ask Dad, "We have to find out." Dad says. We walk down multiple roads, lanes, and streets until we finally reach Eldon Cresent. The name sounds vaguely familiar. And its a cresent-shaped street with an apartment, a shop, a small park, and it's kind of like a community because it has everything. "Why are we here Dad?" I ask him, "Wait here." Dad says and he leaves Bronwyn with us and walks into a small but busy corner shop called 'Harleys'. I remember that store and it has grown a lot bigger since then. Dad comes back 15 minutes later smiling, holding a bar of candy. "I got a job." he says, I sigh with relief. We walk to a small rundown apartment complex and we meet the landlord. The wage Dad gets at the store is 10 pounds per hour. And the rent is 2,100 pounds per month. Dad and the landlord bargain and finally the price is reduced to 1,800 pounds, including the water and electricity bill. I do the quick calculations. It would take Dad 23 days of non-stop working to cover the rent. And we would have only 400 pounds for basic costs. The landlord is a thin man with a pointy nose and thinning blond hair. His name is Mr. Archibald Crumpet. He sniffs, turns on his heels and walks away. Before we entire the flat

I ask Dad, "Dad, I did the calculations. It would take you 23 days to pay off our rent if you work weekdays

because you'll be earning 10 pounds per hour. I can work the weekends. Please dad, let me." I begged him,

"Alright." he says. "I'm going to talk to Mr. Harley now." I say. Suddenly, a memory hits me. I was 11 years

old when I last came to London. Me and Agatha were holding hands and we walked into a shop, with a

bright neon sign 'Harleys.' flashing over head. The same neon sign is there, and the same Mr. Harley. A

man with a big nose, glasses, and wispy white hair. He peers over his glasses as I walk in. "Mr. Harley, Sir."

I say, I explain our situation and try to look desperate. "I already have someone who works during the

weekdays dear," he says gently, he's talking about Dad, for some reason, I try to look surprised about this. I

insist on working weekends and he looks taken aback. "During the weekends? But, but, you possibly

can't-" He says "But I can." I say. He offers 5 pounds per hour and I take it. We fix the time 7AM to 5PM.

With a lunch break from 12PM to 12:30 PM. And I thank him repeatedly until he dismisses me. Today is

Thursday. Day after tomorrow I start working. 5 pounds per hour means, 40 dollars per day. 40 into 8 is

320. So I will be making 320 pounds. I can add that to the 400 for daily costs. So we will have 720 pounds

for daily costs and our rent is covered. I run the rest of the way to the apartment. "I got the job, 5 pounds

per hour!" I burst, Dad hugs me. We lay down to sleep on the cold stone floor that night. Dad left at 9 AM

the next morning. Me, Antonio, and Bronwyn toured the whole community. I took them to the park, and I took them to the pond so we could play stupid made-up games. It was 5 PM, by the time Dad got back home. He got back home 5 cans of soup, and 70 pounds. We gave Bronwyn 2 cans of soup as he was becoming weaker and paler by the day. We cleaned a can of soup and the 70 pounds were placed in the can. We lay down to sleep. Tomorrow is my first day on the job. I woke up at around 6, and I showered got dressed and left to Harleys. I'm nervous and excited. The bright neon sign is not flashing, the shutters are drawn closed. I take in a quick, sharp breath and walk quicker. It's just closed. And then I notice, on the bottom left corner a sticky-taped note. 'hi Yvette. The keys are under the pot plant.' I breathe a sigh of relief and retrieve the keys. I open the shutters and I flick on the switch which indicates Harleys is now open. Mr. Harley walks into the store at 7:03 AM. "Good morning, Mr. Harley." I say, "Good morning, dear." he says grouchily. Our first customer walks in at 7:22 AM. A mousy-looking young man, wearing a cardigan. "I need todays paper, give me the Times." he says, I give him todays copy of the paper and take 3 pounds from the man. A 10p tip. I pocket it and put the 2.50 pound in the cash register. Our next customer is a boy around 7 years old, with many missing teeth. "I want 10 of those." he says pointing to brightly colored hard candy worth 50p each. I give it to him and he gives me 5 dollars which go in the cash register. About half an hour later, an old woman walks up and asks for 4 cabbages, each cabbage worth 1 pound. She give me 4 pounds and 50p. I pocket the 50p and grin at her, "Thank you for the tip, Ma'am!" I say, "No problem dear." she says patting my hand. The day procedes like this and 4 more customers come

in and over all they give me 27 pounds, plus a 2 pounds tip in total. I was just getting bored when 3 high

school girls walk in giggling. 2 of them are blonde. They wore a tremendous load of makeup and high

heels, they carry fancy purses. "Megan, we need this hot pink polish." the shorter blonde cooes to the

brunette. "Yes we do Katie, but first I need the 'Hot Gossip!' magazine!" Megan whines to Katie. "Found

it!" the other blonde squeals and hands it to Megan. "Thank you, Chloe. You really are a gem!" Megan

gushes while flipping through the magazine. She flips it onto the counter, the magazine is 6 pounds, "Now

for the polish." Megan says and examines the hot pink polish worth 2 pounds from before. She sets it on

the counter, "This is a must-have!" she exclaims. They pick up 8 different nail polishes in different shades

of pink and they pick up a bunch of make - up and beauty products. "Thats all, cashier girl." Chloe snarks

to me. I give her a 'whatever smile' and sum up their overall to 156 pounds. Who ever these girls are,

their parents are filthy rich. "Anything else, Ma'am?" I ask. "You wish, cashier girl." Katie says. I put the

156 pounds in the cash register. "No tip Ma'am?" I ask exasperatedly. "Oh," Megan says and reaches into

her purse, these girls aren't as bad as I thought, I think eagerly. She pulls out a bill of air and fakely puts it

on the counter. "There, your tip." she says and all the girls walk out laughing. Stupid, desperate me. I think.

The rest of the day progresses normally with my lunch break and everything. I went home with 40 pounds and 60p. I knock on the door and Antonio answers looking worried. "Whats wrong?" I asked him, "Its Bron, he has a fever." I chill runs down my spine.We have more than enough money to buy the medicine, but we need it for the rent. I walk in a hurry to where Bronwyn lays in Dad's lap. "Oh good, you're back." Dad sighs. "I need you to take all the money that we made, and buy some stuff. Buy a thick blanket, and a thin one. Buy 8 cans of soup, and buy a bottle of medicine for Bron." All this stuff is gonna cost a lot, but I empty out the soup can which has the money and start out in the rain. I caught Mr. Harley just before he was going to shut the store. I told him about everything. And he gave me all the stuff I needed and I gave him the money. I went back home with 85 pounds and put it back in the soup can. "It was 29 pounds. Mr. Harley gave me a discount." I muttered as I lay the thick blanket on the floor, Dad lowered Bronwyn onto it gently and wrapped the thin blanket around him. We fed Bronwyn 2 cans of soup and he refused the third one. Then we gave him medicine and he went to sleep. I drank one can of soup because Mr. Harley gave me a filling lunch of mashed potatoes and chicken stew. Dad and Antonio had 2 cans of soup each and we lay down to sleep again. I woke up late the next morning and I showered, gave Bronwyn his medicine and left. Bronwyn was much better. I was fishing the keys out from the bottom of the pot plant, when Mr.Harley arrived, "Late, today, are we?" he asked quizzicaly, "Sorry, Mr. Harley." I said. "No apology needed," he says with a wave of his hand. It was a regular day with a handful of customers and we got an overall of 194 pounds and I got a tip of 7 pounds and 40p. I bought one small glass bowl, worth 8 pounds

and one steel worth 8 pounds. Then I bought a loaf of bread worth another 10 pounds, and 6 cans of soup

worth 12 pounds. I went back home with all those things, plus, 9 pounds and 40p. We had lesser and

lesser money for rent by the day. But what matters the most, is Bronwyn getting better. "Hey, how's

Bronwyn doing?" I asked Antonio, "Much, much better. The weird thing you gave him worked. And, whats

that?" he asked eyeing the cover. "Bread, soup, utensils." I replied, placing the things on the kitchen

counter. I put the 9 pounds and 40p in the money can. "Hey Dad." I said, Dad was just giving Bronwyn

medicine as I walked in. "I got bread." I offered. "Oh, that wonderful. What else?" He asked, "A steel pot-

pan kinda thingy and a glass bowl for the microwave and the stove." I said, bending down to check

Bronwyn's fever. I could barely even feel the heat. "Why don't you toast the bread, Otter?" Dad asked

planting a kiss on my forehead, "Yeah." I nodded and left. I toasted the bread, and arranged it in the pot-

pan and called everyone for dinner. There was a dining table in the center of the small hall which had 5

chairs, and I put everything on the table. "Mm... Bread." Antonio said, chewing on a burnt piece of toast.

"We've only had 3 days of soup and you guys are already sick of it?" Dad gasped in mock astonishment.

We counted all the money we had left after Bronwyn went to bed, and it was a grand total of 112 pounds.

12 pounds went to daily use and 100 pounds to rent. We all went to sleep with our stomachs content.

Today is Dad's shift, so he left at 8:45. We all avoided breakfast except Bronwyn. For lunch, we had a can of soup each and Bronwyn had a slice of bread. He was getting fussy and irritated, so I ran down to Harleys with 12 pounds and bought a set of 2 toy cars and restocked on 4 cans of soup. I gave Bronwyn the cars, and he gave a happy squeal of excitement. Sunlight poured in unflitered through the entire room, and suddenly, the room spun and I ran out, I steadied myself by gripping the chair. Antonio came running and he gripped my shoulders. "Autumn, are you okay?!" he exclaimed. "I'm so sorry Antonio, I need to go for a walk to clear my head, I feel dizzy." I gasped and stumbled out of the flat. I ran down the stairs all the way and decided to head directly toward the park.

13

The Reunion

A light, cooling drizzle began and it settled my senses. I steadied my breathing as I walked slowly in

the direction of the park, the pavement crunched under my feet. Despite the rains, the sky was a clear

blue and the white clouds were in wisps, trailing across the sky. A wind blew and whipped my hair in

different directions, as I wrapped my arms around myself. As walked on, the grass was a bright green

with dew drops decorating each blade. I heard the sound of some kind of creaking wheel and looked up

thinking it was a bicycle. Instead, I saw a girl who was my age, with blonde hair in a short, hasty crop.

She was thin and had a delicate look about her. She had brownish-golden eyes, and thin pink lips, her skin

sunk around her cheekbones, and her eyes looked a bit hollow. But still, she looked beautiful. Her eyes

widened instantly when she saw me, "Autumn?" her voice was barely audible, just a coarse whisper. "No,"

I whispered back, "Aggie?" I asked running toward her. "Autumn!" her voice rose, I bent down, and enveloped her in a hug. Her nanny gasped, "It's alright, Abigail." Agatha said to her nanny, "She's my best-friend." I teared up instantly. "Aggie," I said, putting a hand on her cheek. "What happened? Where did you go?" I asked, it was true. I went to where they lived before on Pinehurst Gardens. But the tenant said they had vacated 3 years ago. "Come," Aggie said and I walked to bench and she began, gesturing for Abigail to sit down. "I know its not your fault so don't start. But, things took a turn for the worse when you left." she said, I gripped her hand tightly. "Dad stayed with me and Mom for about a month before he went to Ireland on some work. Then Mom went back to her jobs as well. My state got worse and we had to start chemotherapy. Kids bullied me at school, I had no friends. Everything progressed like that for 2 years until we finally cleared all debts. Me, Mom, and Dad went on a trip to Maldives. It was beautiful, I loved it. When we got back home, Dad had to go on some work to Paris. So the flight to Paris was all good. But the flight back from Paris, Dad's company had booked a private plane, and it... Crashed. Or-" I interrupted her, "Aggie, I am so, so, sorry. I can't-" she closed her eyes, and balled her hand into a fist, "Or that's what Dad asked his company to tell us. He was alive, and well. My Mom's friend, Cindy, went to Paris on holiday and she bumped into Dad there. When she told Mom... Mom was heartbroken. With my cancer, Agnes dying, and Dad's whole abandoning us. It, it, it, I just. Mom turned into a workaholic, working 24/7. I only met her once a week and she hired a nanny for me and... Look where I am now." she concluded, I shook my head, "Aggie-" my voice was barely audible, "But everything is fine, because you're back! You're here!"

the color flooded back to her cheeks, "I am." I said nodding. We both looked into the distance, a beautiful

sunset rose over the horizon, "Well Aggs, I'll get going now." I said giving her hand a tight squeeze, she

nodded, she looked so helpless in that wheelchair, I turned away. "Bye, love." she said, "Bye Aggs." I

replied. I heard the sound of the wheelchair being wheeled away. Should I go home? No, I decided. As I

continue to watch, the sunset becomes even more captivating. The sky is a canvas of colors, with the deep

blue gradually giving way to rich purples and soft lavenders. Closer to the horizon, the sky is painted with

brilliant shades of pink and orange, as if the sun has set the clouds on fire. These colors blend seamlessly,

creating a gradient that looks almost surreal. The sun itself is just below the horizon, its last rays stretching

out and casting a gentle glow over the city. The light from the sunset reflects off the glass windows of the

skyscrapers, making them sparkle like jewels. The river captures these reflections, turning the water into a

shimmering mirror that doubles the beauty of the scene. As the daylight fades, the sky becomes a tapestry

of twilight hues, with the first stars beginning to twinkle. The contrast between the cool tones of the

evening sky and the warm, fiery colors of the sunset is striking, making this moment feel both vibrant and

peaceful. The soft breeze carries the faint sounds of the city winding down, adding to the sense of calm

that envelops me as I stand there, lost in the beauty of the sunset. "Wow." I breathed, I slowly walked back from the lake, to back home. Each footstep awakening a new memory with Agatha. Going to Harleys, biking to school, walking in the park, her telling me about Agnes. I shouldn't have left her. I should have convinced my parents to let me stay for one more month. A week, a day, at least?! I felt furious toward myself, I shoved my hands in my pockets. A cold gust of wind blew around, and then, the first sheet of rain poured down. My eyes opened in fear, lightning, thunder, I raced home. This storm is not going to give up soon.

14

Why I Can't Stay

I was soaked thoroughly by the time I knocked on the door at home. The water seeped through,

my shirt, chilling me to the bones. I shivered uncontrollably as Antonio opened the door, I offered

a grin, to which he returned and I raced inside. Dad gave me the thin blanket to wrap around

myself. "I met Agatha." I told Dad and Antonio. "Go for a shower and come, you can tell us what

happened when you get back." Dad instructed, I nodded and gleefully raced into the shower. I tore

my wet clothes of my body and stepped into the hot shower. It warmed me instantly, and I

shuddered for some reason in the warm shower. Maybe it was recalling my nightmare of Agnes' death.

Maybe not. I stepped out of the shower and just straight up wore my jacket from Old Eva. It was

warm and snug. Black tights under. I walked out of the shower and straight to the dining table, Antonio

was heating up a can of soup. "So." Dad asked, "So, I met Aggs at the park. And what she had to tell me was heartbreaking, I swear. You know Aggie's Dad. Carter Stone. And her Mom, Carla Stone. So, Mr Stone

stayed with Aggs and Mrs. Stone for a month before he went to Ireland on some work. Mrs. Stone went

back to her jobs, and... Agatha's condition got worse, they had to start chemotherapy. After 2 years, the

Stones cleared all debts. You remember, don't you Dad? That one time..." It was better not to recall that

memory, but it flooded into my mind. Me, Aggs, Dad, Mom, Mr and Mrs. Stone went for a picnic in the

park. Aggs said she needed to pee, and Mrs. Stone was going with her, when Mom said she had to go too.

Me, Dad and Mr. Stone were eating sandwiches when a man wearing all black, with slicked black hair,

and sunglasses jumped us. He grabbed Mr. Stone by the collar and shook him, I didn't understand what

he was saying because Dad grabbed me and pulled me by the shirt behind a tree, but I saw everything.

Dad rushed out from behind the tree and tried to stop the man, but the man had already punched Mr.

Stone several times and Mr. Stone was bleeding from the mouth. The man slapped Dad and Dad pushed

him to the ground, then picked him up by the collar and slapped him hard. He shoved the man and the

man ran away. The only thing I heard the man say was "You owe us, you little-" and Dad dragged me

away. When Mom, Aggie and Mrs. Stone came back, they saw Mr. Stone's condition and the picnic was

canceled. I felt bad for Mr. Stone then, but definetly not now. "Autumn, Autumn, Autumn!!" Antonio

called me thrice and he waved his hand in front of my eyes, until I snapped out of my daze. "Yeah, yeah, sorry." I glanced at Dad I knew he was thinking the same thing, "Poor Carter. Really didn't deserve it. He

was a good man, hardworking." Dad said shaking his head. "Mr. Stone, was a very bad man. Anyways, after

they cleared their debts, the family went to Maldives. After coming back, Mr. Stone had to go to Paris on

some work. The flight to Paris was perfectly fine. But his company booked a private flight back and well.

It crashed." I said, looking to Dad for a response, "Oh, I don't understand, Otter. Carter was a good-" Dad

said frowning, "*Carter*, asked his company to tell his family that he died. He abandoned them, Dad.

Mrs. Stone's friend, Cindy went to Paris and bumped into him. And... Mrs. Stone became a workaholic,

after finding out about Mr. Stone, she worked 24/7. Aggs only meets her once a week, Dad." I finished, my

voice sounded pained, and my heart throbbed, poor, poor, innocent, naive, lovely, lively, Agatha. "She

didn't deserve this." Dad said exactly what I was thinking.

. . .

Today is Thursday. One day till my shift. I haven't met Agatha since that day. Maybe I'm too scared to

confront her knowing that, I'm not gonna stay in London forever. I don't know why. I was strolling by

the lake the next day, and Agatha was not there. I had a sudden thought. I am not going to stay in

London forever, not for my whole life. I don't know why. But I realized I don't *want* to stay in London

forever. I was always moving, from place to place. Finally when I was going to move from Seattle to San

Diego. I had had enough, Dad and Mom said we could stay in San Diego for 4 years. I was overjoyed!!

We reached San Diego, moved in, unpacked, and in 1 week, we were off to Mexico. All our luggage left at

that hotel. Fresh tears sprung from my eyes as I recalled each happy memory. I don't want to stay in

London. I want to go back to San Diego. The only thing standing in our way of going back to San Diego

was nothing...

Oh wait. There was Agatha.

I thought dimly about her for a second. Was she really worth it? Yes, yes she is. And I better have a talk

with her mother. It was time to talk to Carla Wright.

15

Making Things Right With The Wrights

Agatha had vaguely mentioned that they moved to Heatherton Avenue. And that her Mom would

only come home if there was an emergency and stayed at home after lunch on Sundays. Today is

Monday, not a Sunday. I stormed over all the way to Heatherton Avenue, we were too broke to afford

a taxi or a subway anyways. I was too lost in my thoughts and I bumped into someone, it was a guy,

he looked a little older than me, he had ice-blue eyes, and dark tousled hair. He wore a black hoodie and

had his hands stuck in his pockets. "Are you lost?" he asked smirking, "No." I replied, "Name's Jameson

Whitemore." he said holding out his hand, he had 4 people dressed in similar black trailing after him. I

I could tell playing nice was a good idea, so I extended my hand and said "Yvette Whitlock." "See you

around, Yvette." He said with a wave of his hand, and he was off. His 4 henchmen gave me dirty glares and trailed after Jameson. I sprinted the rest of the way to Heatherton Avenue. I was winded and out of

breath by the time I reached their community. The plaque outside their house said 'Wrights.' I caught my

breath and rang the doorbell. Abigail opened the door looking somewhat flustered and had a pleasant

expression on her face, her face dropped when she saw me. "Oh," she said, frowning, "Its... You." I was

not sure if Agatha had mentioned the name Autumn somewhere during our conversation, but I'm glad

Abigail doesn't remember. She looked displeased and let me in. Aggie was sitting near the dining table

which was massive and had 14 chairs. My eyes almost popped, but I cleared my throat and managed to

make it through this very expensive house without damaging a very expensive object. "Nice house." I said,

Agatha looked up, her face up instantly with joy. "Autumn!" she squeaked, my face coated with alarm,

I turned my head, and Abigail was nowhere in sight. "What's wrong?" Aggie asked worriedly, "Nothing," I

replied smoothly, "Just... Call me, Yvette. Ok?" I said, "OK, Yvette." she said awkwardly. A silence passed.

"I'm so glad you came! I was starting to think that you-" she started, I clutched her hand. It was a pure

impulse to say, "No, never again." She nodded happily. Blissfully ignorant. "Your mom around?" I asked

knowing the obvious answer. "No." she replied. "Well, we need to make her come home," I said firmly.

"B-But why?" she asked, "I need to have a talk, with Ms. Wright," I said.

After 1 hour of pleading, begging, and threatening Abigail finally agreed to the plan. With shaking hands and a trembling voice, Abigail dialed the number and spoke. Here's how their conversation went.

Abigail: "H-Hello? Miss?"

Ms. Wright: Impatiently, "Yes Abigail what is it?"

Abigail: "It's Agatha. She's not responding."

Ms. Wright: "Not responding? What the hell do you mean?

Abigail: "She, she, she." Bursts into tears, "She's dead!!"

Line disconnects and Abigail sniffles and wipes her tears, "There! I did it!!" "Wow, you are really good at

fake crying." I was thoroughly impressed with her acting skills. She burst into tears again, "I'm getting

fired!!" And she fled to her room. 15 to 20 minutes later, a car pulls up in the drive way. And everything is

ready, including my grand speech. Aggs is sitting in her wheelchair at her place at the dining table with me

beside her. The front door slams open and then closed. The clicking of high heels, and the sound of keys

jangling. Her tight bun is a wild mess, her mascara and lipstick are smeared. "What is the meaning of

this?" she asks, "Sit down, Ms. Wright." I said, to my surprise, with worried glances at a nervous Agatha,

Ms. Wright complied. "You must remember me from 6 years ago." I was dead sure she would remember

me but not my name. She had a dazed expression, "I'm not sure I-" "I'm Yvette Whitlock. I was Aggie's

friend in fourth grade. We had gone for that picnic...?" I prompted, "Ahh, yes. I remember." she said,

nodding vigorously. I held Agatha's hand, I spoke softly, "Agatha is not dead on the outside, but she is

on the inside, Ms. Wright." Ms. Wright's eyes darted between me and Agatha. "You and Mr. Stone were always busy with work. Agnes was like a mother to her. And because of your irresponsibility, she died.

That's when Aggie died for the first time. Next when Mr. Stone did what he did. And what Mr. Stone did is

no different from what you are doing right now, Ms. Wright." Ms. Wright's eyes widened, then narrowed,

"Listen here, Yvette. I don't know who you think you are-" she snarked, pointing her finger at me. "No, Ms.

Wright!" I screamed, "What you are doing is wrong!!" she looked startled and drew her hand back, "You,

have abandoned your only daughter!! You meet her once a week! What kind of mother are you?! Do you

have any idea what she's going through?!" I yelled, tears were pouring out of my eyes rapidly. "You are no

different from Mr. Stone! You abandoned her using work as an excuse!! What are you so scared of?!" I

wiped my eyes furiously, and smoothed down my hair "I hope you have a better relationship in the near

future with your daughter, Ms. Wright." I gave Aggs a smile, I squeezed her hand, and said, "Bye, Aggie!"

"Bye. Love." she called softly after me. Ms.Wright followed me to the door looking befuddled and

dumbstruck. "I'm sorry," she whispered. "Not to me, but to your daughter." I whispered back and patted

her shoulder comfortingly. The whole while back home I thought about Ms. Wright, Agatha, and my

encounter with Jameson. Dad said be home before 4 where ever you are except on Saturdays and Sundays

of course. I'm late, its already 3:40. I checked on someone's phone. Worst Dad could do was ground me

right?? But the crowd was dispersing slowly, a few weird-looking people came out of alleyways. The sun was setting, no! Don't go! I begged the sun, but of course, it didn't listen. I quickened my walk to a sprint,

and I was still 20 minutes away from home when a black car pulled up in front of me. I was too busy

looking around, but I heard a familiar voice,"Need a ride?" I got into the car without looking, stupid of me,

really. I gave a short puff of breath, and looked up to see Jameson looking at me with an amused

expression. He pushed his hair out of his eyes, "Uh... I'm sorry, I'm not really from around here. I was-" I

started, "That is a dangerous area after 3:30, 4. Best not go there." he said and turned away, his jaw set.

Who was this guy? With his weird mood changes? I turned away too. We stopped outside the apartments.

"Thanks for the ride, Jameson," I said, he just nodded. I shut the door and walked off.

16

Recap.

It was April when Mom died. Oh, that bittersweet month. It was the 7th of April to be precise.

4th was when we moved to San Diego. I had to no time to enjoy the sweet fruits of the tree that

had been cut down to fast. It is August now. Sorry for fast-forwarding so many months ahead. Here are

a few updates.

- - -

➡?Aggie is getting better, and her Mom spends a lot more time with her.

➡?Me, Jameson, and Aggie are best friends now.

➡?Bronwyn is 2 years old, he turned 2 in May.

➡?Antonio got a job as a gardener at Lady Cavandish's mansion. He gets paid 2,000 per month...

And... Yeah. So don't get mad at me. My life is pretty boring, with a dash of excitement when Jameson

and Aggie come in. So, it's just perfect. With me, Dad, Bronwyn, and Antonio.

17

The Really Unnecessary Questions

I stormed angrily over to our meeting spot, where I knew Jameson would be. He leaned against a grand oak, hands firmly in his pocket. "You look rainy today Raine," he said, Oh yeah. . . My name is Autumn Raine Winchester. "Oh shut up." I growled back, "Why the thunderclouds?" he teased, "Is it going to rain, Raine?" "Jamie, actually shut up. I'm not here for chit-chat. I'm here to talk about you." I said, Jameson plopped himself down on the ground, "Well, I'm ready to listen." He said pushing the hair out of his eyes.

"What's wrong with you?" I asked sitting in front of him, "Nothing and everything at the same time." he replied smirking, I sighed, always the same with James. "You always speak in riddles, and, and, and, whats with those sudden mood changes? And when we're around your people, you always act different, like a cold-hearted introvert." I asked, Jamie's face darkened. "Autumn. Don't ask me these kind of questions."

"Stop avoiding these questions, James." Jamie took in a deep breath, "You know I don't always speak in

riddles, Raine." his voice dragged like I was sucking every bit of life from him by asking these questions.

"I'm going to tell you a secret. And to some people, it might seem stupid and non - believable, but I know

not to you. People like us are never satisfied, we don't get happily ever afters. That's a fact you would have

realized by now." He said, I had, I had realized it long ago. I stayed silent. "My Dad runs the biggest mafia

all around the US and the UK." he paused, waiting for a reply. "I believe you. Jamie." I said in a reassuring

tone. He nodded, "Since I was a year old, I've been trained, rigorously to be heartless. Because a mafia

must never lose his heart to anyone. Must show no signs of emotions to anyone. But that doesn't work

with me!! I don't want to be someone who lives in the dark and keeps people in the dark!! I don't want to

become the embodiment of darkness, Raine!" his voice broke, "I don't want to be this, this, this, monster,

that they want me to be. But I have to. Raine. I have to, or they'll kill me, they'll kill us all." his voice

turned ragged. "I'm sorry, I didn't mean to go there." I said, "It was about time." He snapped. "I know," he

hissed, "I know you don't intend to stay in London forever. Good. Because friendship with me, will only

cause anyone outside the mafia pain. So forget about London and never look back again." "Jameson, you

don't have to be the person they-" I started, "But I do!! I'm a Whitemore. We always want more, and more.

And more!! Raine. No one can fix me, not you, not anyone, not god. You can't fix me!! So forget about everything I told you Raine, and leave while you can." He said getting up, taking the dagger out of his belt,

"I'm not leaving," I replied firmly, I was not going anywhere. "I am," he said, glaring at me, and stalked off.

He would be back tommorow, I know it. I stood up and swaggered back to the apartments. Jameson, if

only you could see. . .

18

Dreaming Big.

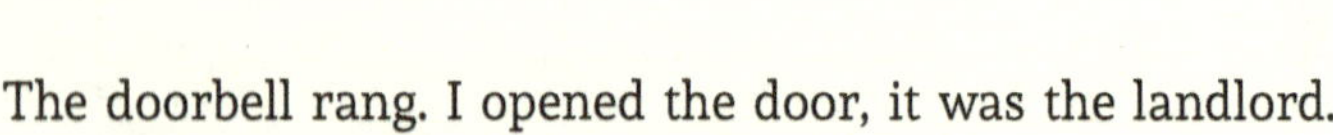

The doorbell rang. I opened the door, it was the landlord. Archibald. He looked eager, "The rent?" he peeped meekly. I gave him a bored look, "Mr. Crumpet. I've already told you this before. Not a day before the actual date of the rent. The first of every month. Mr. Crumpet it is only the 19th of August!! This is unacceptable!! Too much!! Reduce our rent by 1,000 or we will report you!!" I blubbered, "I, I, I am sorry, Yvette. I will be back on 1st." he looked like he bit on a bug. "As expected. Good day!" I trilled and slammed the door on his pathetic face. Ugh. I loathe people who love money that much. I didn't get to report Octavia and Serphina. But Jose did, and we read in the paper that they were arrested. We gave Mr. Crumpet money one week before the rent date and he took money again from us on rent day!! We threatened to report him but he's just as bad, Ugh. I wore my wellies and my raincoat and prepared to go out. To our usual meeting spot, I stepped in the puddles of rain and looked at my reflection. I reached our spot, where was Aggie? And James? I turned around to leave when someone pulled at my wrist with a firm

grasp. I turned, "Jameson? Whats wrong?" I asked, to a winded, out-of-breath Jameson, he brushed his hair

away with his hands "Hey, Raine." He said. "I told Dad. I didn't want to be a criminal, a mafia boss. He held

a knife, to Paisley's throat, a drop of blood fell here, right here." He said pointing to a faded spot of red on

his hand. I gasped, "Paise..." she was a sweet, innocent, little girl. A lot like Aggs. "Is she okay?" I croaked,

only 7-year-old Paisley. "Yeah. That monster, he didn't kill her, Rai." he said. A teardrop escaped my eye,

"This is all my fault, Jameson. If I hadn't told you..." I trailed off, Jameson held a dagger to his own throat,

"Jameson!!" I shrieked, I slapped the dagger away from him and then slapped him. "Have you lost your

mind?!" I yelled. "I will do it, if you say one more word about it being your fault. Ugh. It disgusts me,

Raine. I should take the responsibility now. Own up to my mistakes." he said producing another knife

from his belt. "Not your mistakes." I corrected him and sat down on the grass, he sat beside me. "I'm sorry,

Raine. Sometimes the training kicks in in the wrong way. I'm not supposed to do the right thing with my

training." he said, I sighed. Why was I trapped in this web? I want to leave. I don't want to leave my

best friends, Jamie and Aggie. I want them to come with me. "Let's leave then!!" I announced, "Where?!"

He said equally as loud. "Anywhere but here!" I yelled back, "Let's leave, Jameson, You, me, Aggie, Dad,

Bron, Antonio, Paisley, Arlo. Let's get away from this wicked place." Jameson tilted his head like an confused puppy and smirked, with an amused expression. "Big dreams, Rai." with that he got up and

strolled off, whistling to himself. "Its up to me then, to make those dreams a reality, Jameson Whitelock."

"We'll see about that. Autumn. Raine. Winchester." his voice echoed in my head.

19

The Warning

I took the train to Agatha's house, I rang the doorbell, and Ms. Wright answered she looked at me and

looked pleased instantly. "Hi, sweetheart! Me and Aggie were just baking cookies!" I beamed back. I gave

Ms.Wright a hug. I liked her now. I gave a flour-coated Aggie a hug too, her long, luscious locks were

growing back. Abigail hadn't changed, she still looked disappointed to see me. "Why didn't you come

yesterday and the day before?" I asked Aggs, "Oh, I went to the movies day before, and I was under the

weather yesterday." she flushed a bright red. Fair enough "I hope you're feeling better?" she nodded,

adding a dash a of milk in this, a pinch of sugar in that. We put the cookies in the oven to bake. And settled

down, we did a little bit of chit chat and the cookies were ready to be eaten, they were absolutely

delicious!! After my stomach was full, I told Ms. Wright that if Aggie didn't come to the meeting spot

tommorow I would be forced to kidnap her, and Ms. Wright said she was fine with that. I left not soon after. I wanted to walk home, the weather was good, calm. After 15 minutes, I felt someone following me, it was a squat bald man, with barely a few strands of blonde hair. He had rabbit teeth and was flushing a bright red. I turned and walked quicker, another man followed, he was taller and had curly, black hair, he had a mole on the top of his lip and wore a nose ring. I walked faster and so did they. Great. I have a tail. I heard the sound of a weapon being cocked. I ran. I ran like my life depended on it because it did. "Hey!!" a voice growled, "Stop right there you!" another screamed. I was not going to stop, no way!! Home was only 2 minutes away if I ran. These were mafia people. I couldn't lead them right to Dad, Bronwyn and Antonio. So I stopped and pulled out my phone, and called Jameson. He picked up, "James, there are two people following me! Tell them to get lost." I hissed, I held the phone up for them to. "Pablo! Picasso! I knew it was you, you filthy scoundrels! Get back!!" Jameson shouted over the phone. The pair passed me dirty looks and fled, like wounded puppies. I breathed a sigh or relief. "Raine..." Jameson was still on line. "I'm sorry." he said, "It's dangerous, it's not okay. Jamie." I replied, "I warned you." he replied and the line disconnected after I didn't reply. I knocked on the door and Antonio answered. I must have looked pretty flustered, "Are you okay?" Antonio asked, "Yeah, I'm fine. Just, a little winded, I guess." I said with a small smile which he didn't return. He just took in a deep breath. He was getting sick and tired of me, and my lies, everyone was. I sighed too. I wanted to come clean to him. Poor Antonio. So wise, but still treated like a toddler. I watched as the first raindrops pelted the window incessantly. I took a gulp of breath, "Antonio,

we have to leave London." And then I told him everything. He took it well, and then nodded. "Right, so,

Autumn?" he asked, "Yeah?" I replied. "I have a plan." He said firmly.

20

The Plan

We waited till Dad got home, and I told him everything. Then Antonio explained the plan(s). Of course

there were two options.

Op. 1 - We move out of our flat and collect all the money for 1 month, and then buy tickets with some

money for, the four of us plus, Jameson, Paisley, and Arlo. Oh, and Aggs. And use the rest of the money to

settle in the new place we're going to.

Op. 2 - We stay in the flat but cut down on several things, take the same people. Ask Aggie to pay for her

own ticket, but will have less money as savings to settle into our new home.

We are looking at Germany. It is the shortest distance from here. After thinking we all decide that Op.2

would be better. Why? Well, the truth is. I know she won't come, I know Aggie will not come with us by

any chance, no way. She missed her mother for 8 years and it was almost like there was a random woman

living with her all these years. And Ms. Wright would never come with us to Germany leaving all her riches and assets behind, and the mafia doesn't know that Agatha is Jameson's friend, and its better it stays that way. Thinking all of this I pushed the protruding thought to the back of my mind. I would have to leave Agatha again. And this time I had no choice. I pushed that thought to a corner making sure it would never surface again.

21

Fast Fwd a Month

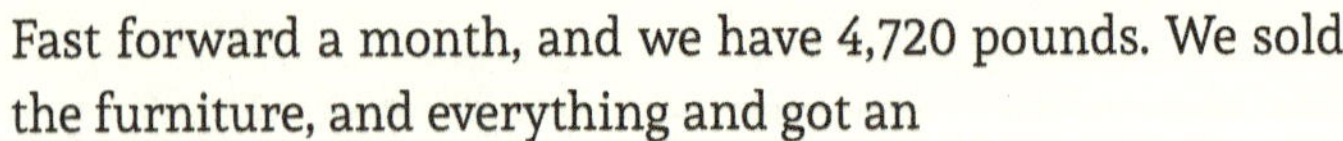

Fast forward a month, and we have 4,720 pounds. We sold the furniture, and everything and got an additional 325 pounds. So a total of 5,045 pounds. I did the euros conversion and we would have 5,958 euros. The birds are chirping, the weather is sunny and-No its not. The clouds look as heavy as ever as I stepped into the park. I gave a sideways glance at my surroundings. Ever since that encounter with 'Pablo' and 'Picasso.' I haven't seen Jameson often. Only a few brief meetings where all we exchanged was eye contact. I'm hoping to see him today. "Did you make those dreams come true, Raine?" a voice teased from on top of an Alder tree, I gaped at him, "How did you?-" he jumped down, smirking. "I think we can leave today? Raine?" He asked, "Bought the tickets." I replied hoarsely. He raised his eyebrows, "How much do we have left..?" he lingered on that question "4,425 pounds." I said. Jameson sighed, "What is it?" he asked begrudgingly, "I can't just leave her again, can I Jameson?" I burst, "It's not like you want to is it Raine?" he said equally as loud, "But I do!! I want to leave London behind and everything about it execpt you and her

but she won't come. Not when she finally has someone... And its wrong for us to try and make her leave."

I said weakly, my voice dying down. "Sit down." Jameson said, "I've got to tell you something." I sat

impatiently. "Why do I want to leave London, Rai?" Jameson asked, "Do you know?" Yes. Obviously, I

knew. "To escape the mafia and your dad. And-" "Thats one of the reasons. I want to protect my siblings

and I want to have a story to tell. Raine. When one day someone asks me, 'Mr. Whitemore, what is the

reason for your success?' I want to be able to tell my story." He stops, "Listen, Raine. Everyone has a story,

including you. Right, even the lowly-est of scums have a story about how they ended up on the street.

And those rats, Pablo and Picasso, they have a story too. So does my dad, your dad, Agatha, Ms. Wright.

My story should be one to tell, Raine." he concluded. "Dad's gonna kill me anyways, so I'll start

somewhere fresh." he said, I gave him a sad smile, "I made the dream come true, didn't I? Jamie?" I asked

softly. "Thank you." He said, and he was gone.

.

I knew, for sure what I was going to do next.

22

A Little Too Close.

I don't know how I got here, or when I did, but I stood on Agatha's front porch, completely

winded and out of breath. I rang the doorbell and Abigail answered looking as nice as ever. Before

she could speak I barged my way in and walked straight to Agatha's room, and pushed in without

knocking. Agatha, in a rocking chair. Bald head, hollowed cheekbones, pale skin, sunken eyes, her

fragile frame even worse. I rushed to her side. The last I saw her she looked plumper, eyes full of life,

pink lips, her blonde hair in a hasty cut at her shoulders. But beautiful. "Agatha?" I exclaimed. Her

eyebrows rose, "Yvette?" she croaked, I took her hands. I barely had time to splutter a what, when, where

who, and why, before she asked, "I thought you left again, Eve." "I was right here." I whispered, "Whenever

I came by, Abigail always said you were not home." "Abigail, never told me you came. Help me." she hissed,

"What?" I asked, "Please, it's Mum. She won't let me leave her sight. Before it used to be fun, spending time and everything, but now? She won't let me leave the house, Yvette." she croaked. What had I done?

"Aggs, aggs, aggs, sweet, lonely, kind, Aggs. Please, please, please, come with us. We're going to Germany, away from London. Me, Dad, Antonio, Jamie, Arlo, Paisely. And, we're running short on money but you can surely afford it? It's 50 pounds, Aggie." I pleaded, she shook her head. "I can fix her, Eve. Believe me, I can." "No, I'm sorry. There are bigger problems than your psychotic mother, Agatha!" I snapped, she was taken aback. I continued in a gentler tone, "Aggie, she's been crazy, she's always been crazy. No one can fix her I'm sorry. I want a better life for you. For us. Please." "Yvette. Going to Germany, would mean leaving me. Once again." Agatha closed her eyes and unleashed the ultimatum. Great. "Aggs, please, there are bigger problems. We could die, if we stayed here any longer. We-" I started. "Yvette. I need some water, fetch me some please?" she asked, "Uhm sure." I left the room. I came back with a glass of water, she handed me a baby pink envelope. "Bye, Evie." she said handing me the envelope, the envelope was bulging, "Go now, and never come back. It's for your best. And mine." she said under her breath, she gripped my wrist pulled me down, and planted a kiss on my cheek. Her eyes brimmed with tears. I kissed her on the forehead. "Bye. Love." she called after me, "You're the one who broke my heart for the last time." She said.

I heard the click of high heels in the hallway and turned to face Ms. Wright. Tears were running down my cheeks. "You monster." I hissed at her, and I ran. I never looked back. I took the taxi back because I couldn't trust myself to walk.

23

Innocent Blood is Drawn.

I opened the envelope only when I got home. It contained 2000 pounds. And a note. Disbelief shook me

and I did nothing to stop it. I opened the note with shaking hands,

Dear Autumn,

(I'm sorry 'Yvette', I can't pretend. . .) I'm thankful, and sorry. To you, if not to anyone.

I know you have to leave, and I can't stop it. But please. If you're going to keep coming

into my life again and again, to break me, don't come. Leave. It's for your best. And mine.

With lots of love,

Agatha. XOXO.

My heart shattered with each word as I understood the reality of my decision. I can't act on impulse.

Pros and cons. I ran them over in my head. But leaving Aggie when her condition was so. . . The

room was spinning, I gripped the edge of the bed. I was teetering over a mountain of regrets. All the noises, the cars from outside, people yelling, settled into a steady high-pitched hum. Like a kettle. About to explode. My breath was becoming labored. Dad came in, the humming stopped, I lifted my head to look at him. He wore a worried smile, "You okay, Otter?" He asked, sitting down beside me, his brows knitted in worry. "Fine," I replied, my knuckles white from gripping the bed so hard. Dad took both my hands, "I'm so sorry, I'm not fulfilling my role as a father. You take care of everything, Autumn. I am forever indebted to you, my love. I'm so sorry, everything I do, everywhere I go. I, I, I can't stop thinking about her." he says. "Dad," is all I can muster. He smiles at me and begins to leave, "Dad, can you buy the tickets for, um, day - after - tommorow?" I ask him, I want to remember London as much as I can.

"Of course." the corners of his eyes crinkle as he smiles.

...

I'm wrapped in a brown coat that comes till my knees, complete with black leggings, and a white t-shirt.

I'm passing an alleyway, and I see a couple of blue eyes. That startles me and I walk faster. Something cold closes over my mouth and a hand grabs both of my hands behind my back, I'm dragged into the alley.

I turn to face Jameson. His meticulously styled black hair a mess, his blue eyes are overcome with fright and anger, there is blood on his hands, then I realize that there is blood on my face. He has a wild and perturbed look on his face. "Jamie?" I ask and step closer to him, he moves back defiantly. "Who's blood-" my voice quivers only fearing the worst, "Paisley. Arlo." he whispers, his eyes drop to the ground, and his head hangs. "Paisley, and Arlo?" I can't believe my ears. Paisley and I thought I could take something

that innocent with me, she was only 7 years old. And Arlo? He was 5. "Jamie, really?" my voice breaks,

"They had a good life, Autumn," he says, slumping down against a wall, I shimmy up beside him. "They

didn't, Jameson. And its all my fault. Its my fault I convinced you to stand up to them, its my fault they

died Jameson. I should leave. I'll get you the money, run away. Somewhere else, somewhere far from

me." I said getting up and backing away, I was dangerous. It was me all along, I took in a sharp breath.

Just as I turned around, his hand gripped mine, and his fingernails dug into my hand. "Please, please,

please, Raine." he murmured in a strained voice, "Who do I have left? Other than you, Adam, Bronwyn,

and redhead?" Redhead was what Jameson called Antonio. "If we split ways it means I did all this for

nothing. It means alot. It means Paise and Arlo died for nothing." his voice cracked. He put his head

between his knees, and his hands over his head. And he began sobbing, his whole frame shook with those

sobs. I sat beside him, one hand clutching his, one hand pressed on my forehead. "Tommorow we leave,

Jamie. I promise." I said.

24

When The Time Comes.

"Ready?" I ask Dad.

"Ready."

"Now?"

"Soon," Dad replied.

If someone asked me the same thing I would say 'never.' Because I'm never going to be ready after what happened. We sit in our now empty apartment, marks on the floor where our furniture was. We have 20 pounds handy and 5, 959 euros. We all await the time. It won't come.

.

But, oh, it does. Our doorbell rings. None of us moved a muscle, I find myself holding my breath. Antonio answers the door. And outside is a flustered Jameson. "Adam, Redhead." he says exchanging nods with Dad and Antonio. He leaves his suitcase, picks up a wide-eyed Bronwyn, and twirls him around till the world won't stop spinning. Twirling or no twirling, the world never stops spinning for me. "Ready to leave?" I ask the party reluctantly. Everyone stares at me with mixtures of emotions. Dad, with sadness and admiration and love. Jameson, with trust and gratefulness and thankfulness. Antonio, with a warm smile, and consideration and belief. And finally, Bronwyn, with utter, utter, confusion. And, I. Look back into each of their eyes respectively, with reluctance, pity, and reassurance. Dad gets up, "Alright people. Lets get this show on the road." Oh - so - optimistic. You know, at least he trys. Look at me. You don't see my trying. he rubs his hands fervently. We each grab our suitcases and head out the door. "Mr. Crumpet," Antonio says as we bump into him in our last turn to the exit. "Liam, Gatsby, Yvette. Where are you guys going? Not planning to leave are you?" Archibald Crumpet, our landlord says with a light, breezy laugh, meant to be followed after a joke. All of our faces remain serene. "Oh, you really are?" his eyes go wide, he lifts his finger up in objection. "Yes, we are. Mr. Crumpet. So, could you please, uh, step aside?" Dad says dismissivley. "Now just hold on Mr. Whitlock. I think we could talk about this, our apartments are so beautiful. Our flats so sufficient. Why don't you stay a while longer?" he hollered after us, I gave him a look of pity over my shoulder. He stood there looking defeated, he stared after us, blinked twice, hard. Pointed his nose to the sky, turned on his heels abruptly and walked away. Suitcase in one hand, briefcase in another Jameson whistled to himself as he strolled ahead of us. The airport was 1 hour away, Stanrow International Airport of London. Living in Germany was going to be hard, the language, the weather, everything. But right now? Anything to get away from London and its memories.

And. . .

Everything about it.

25

Freeze.

The 5 of us piled into a taxi and there was barely enough space. Not soon after the journey started heavy raindrops, full of remorse, pelting the windows as if they were in a hurry to get away. I pressed my cheek to the cold glass, and I noticed Jameson. He was turning his head side to side. Checking my window his, the rear windows Dad's windows, the drivers windows. We exchanged a brief glance, "Tail," he murmured, then raised his voice. "We've got a tail!!" Dad pushed an extra 10 pound bill into the drivers hands, "I need to drive." Dad said, he wore a concerned expression. The driver stalled the car and they clambered over each other, Bronwyn was fast asleep on Antonio. Dad shook himself and the driver whose name tag we now had a glimpse of had the name Freddie on it. Freddie looked absolutely perplexed, he said a quick prayer, he looked between Dad and the bill and decided the bill was better. He gulped, "Okay Jameson," Dad said, "Where are they?" "Three cars behind us on the right, its the black car." Jameson replied, of course, this car had no number plate. "It's the car with no license plate, Dad." I told Dad. Dad swerved right, and Freddie gave a squeak of defiance. Then right once more, the car was still on our tail, much closer now. Picasso was driving, Pablo beside him was smiling ominously. "Those damned rats." Jameson cursed under his breath. I was on the edge of my seat, Dad swerved right one more time. Freddie passed out. And the car swerved out of our view. I breathed a sigh of relief. A black car pulled up beside us, and the windows rolled down slowly, each ticking second, a skipping heartbeat. He had slicked black hair, and those unmistakable blue eyes. Anyone would think that was Jameson when he was a grown-up. Jameson looked exactly like his Dad. His eyes widened, and Jameson. He just froze. "Grayson Whitemore." that's the name Jameson once told me. Grayson Whitemore. Their car pulled up ahead of us, blocking our path.

We couldn't go back because Pablo and Picasso's car was behind our car. Mr. Whitemore smirked, an unmistakable smirk. "My son, this little escapade has been fun enough, but I think its time we go home," he purred. Jameson blinked hard, once, twice, thrice, "No." he said. "No?" Mr. Whitemore let out a little chortle. "What makes you think you have an option? James?-" just as he was about to continue, Jameson cut him off with a wave of his hand. "Don't call me that." He snarled back. How could the both of them be so similar, yet so different? That if they were to collide, the most disastrous thing would happen.

Jameson turned to the window, gritting his teeth and clenching his fists. While Mr. Whitemore, smoothed down his shirt and maintained a coherent exterior. I sighed, and began to speak against myself. "Look, Mr.

Whitemore-" I began "Yvette don't." Jameson hissed, I ignored him. "We just-" I started again, "Yvette,

Yvette, please." he pleaded with me. "Need to get somewhere. And Jameson is practically a grown-up now.

I think we can manage ourselves, we have a grown man with us. So please, get out of the way." I said

through gritted teeth. He laughed a pleasant laugh, "No." he said, "No, Jameson. It is your destiny your past

your present, and your future. You don't have another choice. Whenever and wherever you go, this is the

destiny that will follow you, boy. It is your family legacy, and the legacy that beholds you. Your father,

your grandfather, and your forefather all fulfilled this destiny in some way or another. And," he drawled

lazily, "So will you. You and me, we're not made for this little life, we're made for something so much

bigger, and better, and greater!" he exclaimed, his voice rising dangerously. "Jameson, *Jameson.* Come

home now, its for the better of you, my child. Make your story, forge your path, become *someone.* You

have a chance for all that, just come, with me." he said, reaching out of the window, just a hand - length

away, Jameson could take his hand. "No." Jameson said simply, "I will forge my own story, my own destiny,

I will be my own someone. I can do it, I learnt from you after all." He snapped sarcastically Mr. Whitemore

recoiled his hand as if someone burnt him, "My poor child don't make this mistake, or I will have to end

you, just the way I ended *them.* Now we wouldn't want that, would we?" he growled menacingly, I gasped, what kind of father was he? A terrible one, that is. "I'd like to see you try." Jameson said his eyes flashing in the same unmistakable way, "Oh try I will. You may be on your way now, but rest assured I will track you down wherever you are, whenever, however. Go. Run. But if I find you, you have to come with me and take your rightful place as the heir to this spectacular kingdom. If I don't find you, you can waste your life however you want. So now, go. Go as far as you want. You can run, my son. But you can't hide." With those final words as a deathblow, Mr. Whitemore cackled and sped away. Atleast one problem decided to leave, I knew it was going to come back to haunt us again. But for now, we were fine. Dad drove, drove like he thought Mr. Whitemore was suddenley going to change his mind and come after us. Drove because he wanted us to get on that flight to Germany. Drove, for us, if not for anyone. And there was Jameson, he didn't utter a word for the rest of the drive. Antonio finally broke the piercing silence, "Well," he announced, "This is the terminal, Uncle Adam." We got off the car, took our luggage and dad opened the front - row passenger door, and shook Freddie by the shoulder. "Um, Freddie? Freddie, Freddie!" He woke up with a surprised snort, then looked at the five of us standing in the door way, squealed and jumped in his seat. He unfastened his seat belt with fumbling fingers while all of us watched with amusement. He pulled down his window and squeaked a 'thank you!' before speeding away.

26

Orange Juice

"Passengers of the flight from London to Germany. Final boarding call." Came the announcement.

"Why'd you choose such a horrible airline? I mean, the service is so bad." Jameson whined, he finally

started talking again. He said he was done, done thinking about his Dad and the mafia. And none of

us were going to think about it if he wasn't. Our flight is at 9PM. I'm surprised he's even awake. Bronwyn

walked over to a dustbin, tripping over his own feet, in his hands he crushed a juice box. Orange juice

dribbling down his chin and hands. "Shouldn't we get going?" Antonio asked nervously, "Nah," Jameson

replied, "Nothing but a crowd right now." he said jerking his thumb back to the line of the passengers

waiting to board our flight. 10 minutes later, all of us strolled casually to the entryway. Knowing that no

line awaited us. I relaxed a little after looking at the pleasant flight attendants' face, maybe there was no

reason to worry. I scanned the rest of the passengers in the flight, and took in a deep breath. And took in another. My seat was 9A. Dad's and Bronwyns were 3E and 3D. Antonios and Jameson's seats were 17A

and 17B. In the middle seat of my row, sat a timid-looking woman, in her mid 20's or 30's. She wore a

floral patterned dress, and leggings, with a purple sweater. All she carried with her was a sparkly, red

handbag, an odd mix and match of colors. I wanted to talk to her, I decided. "Um, Hi. I really like your

handbag." she looked startled, then she beamed. "Oh, thank you. I found this old thing in a dollar store,

and, I, managed to fix it up. My name's Millie, by the way." she said. "My name's Yvette. Yvette Whitlock,

do you live in Germany, or . . . ?" I asked, "Oh no, I don't." she replied with a pleasant laugh, "I'm just an

English teacher. My sister lives in Germany, with her husband. She's pregnant, and her baby is due in a

week. And I haven't met her in 2 years, so I decided to stay with them for awhile." "Oh, that must be hard,

not being able to meet your sister for 2 years." I replied, "We connect over Facetime but yeah, it is. What

about you? Flying with your parents?" She asked, "My Dad, my brother, and my cousins. My mom. . . Um,

she passed away," I gulped, "I'm so sorry," Millie said, she laid a hand on my hand. Then she smiled, "Tell

you what, Sweetheart. I think I have just the thing to cheer you up." and with that, she started rummaging

in her handbag, she produced a Weather's Original toffee, and handed it to me. "Thank you," I said gladly,

and popped the toffee in my mouth. "This used to be my favorite, when we used to live in London when I

was 9. We keep moving, yeah? Can't seem to decide on one place." I said, sucking on the toffee. Millie, nodded, still smiling. "Alright, then Yvette. I think I‘m gonna take a quick nap, I woke up at 4AM today. The

cats just wouldn’t stop making noise." She said tiredly, putting on her eyemask, and her neckpillow. Yeesh.

Cats. They terrify me. But of course I didn’t say anything. Next to Millie sat a, boy. I’m guessing, 8 to 11

years old. He didn’t care about anybody’s business except his own. He had his headphones in, and was

busy on his iPad. Oh well. I decided I did not want to talk to him. I wanted to sleep, and I was so tired. But

so restless. I turned my head side-to-side, to the aile, to the window. And settled at looking out the

window. I was going to miss the light London drizzle, forever ready to remind you of your sorrows and

misery. Ugh. Why did I have to be so depressing? Depressed or not, I am going to miss London. I sighed

as the first raindrops pattered the windows gleefully.

"Attention all passengers, my name is Captain Archie.

I‘m assissted my co-captain Oliver. The flight attendants who will be assisting us today are, Samantha,

Lucille, Bethany, and Priya. Please fasten your seatbelt at all times, if there is any need of assistance press

the button above and a flight attendant will assist. In case of any medical emergency, we have first - aid

kits and a doctor aboard. Our flight is estimated to land in 1 and hours, or 2 hours if there is turbulence,

Thank you for choosing our airlines, have a pleasant journey. Thank you." the Captain turned the mic off

with a click. And then a female voice in German, "Die Flugbegleiter, die uns heute unterstützen werden,

sind: Samantha, Lucille, Bethany und Priya. Bitte schnallen Sie sich immer an. Wenn Sie Hilfe benötigen, drücken Sie Klicken Sie auf die Schaltfläche oben und ein Flugbegleiter wird Ihnen behilflich sein. Im

Falle eines medizinischen Notfalls haben wir Erste Hilfe Ausrüstung und ein Arzt an Bord. Unser Flug

wird schätzungsweise in einer Stunde landen, bei Turbulenzen in zwei Stunden. Vielen Dank, dass Sie

sich für unsere Fluggesellschaft entschieden haben. Wir wünschen Ihnen eine angenehme Reise. Danke

schön." I closed my eyes, I couldn't sleep like this, not with the constant whine of the engine. I pressed

the button for the flight attendant. After a few seconds a flight attendant padded with soft footsteps to my

seat. I read her name tag in the dim light, 'Priya.'. She had a creamy, chocolate brown skin, and bright eyes.

Her thick, black hair was braided down her back. "Hi. Can I help you?" she asked, "Um, yeah. Can I have

earplugs, please?" I asked, motioning to my ears. "Of course." and with that she was gone, a minute later,

she came back with a set of pink earpugs in a plastic cover and handed them to me, "Here you go.". I

accepted them gratefully, "Thank you." She smiled at me and left. I sighed and unwrapped the cover, the

plugs were soft and surpsingly squishy. I put them on and settled into a restless slumber.

27

A Thing of the Past

I woke up with a jerk, and a faint voice echoed through the chaos, "Passengers, please calm down. You

might die, so please." that was the captain's voice, what was happening? I couldn't make out the faces of

the people around me. Everyone was standing, yelling and screaming, and the plane was swaying so much

that everyone was gripping something to be able to stand. One boom of thunder, and one crash of

lightning sent the plane into the murky abyss of water below. I craned my neck to catch a glimpse of Dad,

or Bronwyn. Antonio or Jameson. Anyone. Only a bunch of dark silhouettes shrieking. The water seeped

in through the plane. It soaked up my shoes, and suddenly. The floor beneath me gave in, and I dropped

into the water. It was cold, chilling to the very bones. Above me was the plane, in the plane was water. I

couldn't swim up. I couldn't swim around the plane because it was too long. I screamed as loud as I

could as the last air bubble left my mouth. The last I remember was the ghostly, pale face of a woman. Her features were strikingly familiar, too familiar. Even. I woke up gasping for air. All I saw around me was

darkness, and it was cold. I was in the cold arms of someone. I was also still in the water. I pushed away

from whoever it was. And I got a good look at her face. Mom. Of course, it was Mom. "Mom?" my voice

bubbled from my throat as I choked back tears. She reached toward me nodding, extending her hand. With

her other hand, she caressed my face. But my hand stayed limp at my side. "Lets go, lets go up. Lets live

our lives together. My shining silver star." her voice rasped, her eyes looked eager. No, wrong word. They

looked desperate. I took her hand as the desperation got the best of me too. But as we both swam too the

surface, something pulled me down. I glanced at Mom. Her leg was entangled in the seaweed. No, not

again. Not finally when I have the chance to be with her. I felt suffocated as I watched her struggle, I felt...

Short of breath. My air was running out. My *time* was running out. Something was pulling me up. Mom

was pulling down. I felt like I was going to burst, stretch into a million pieces and then just. . . Burst.

"Mom," I strained, "I can't breath. Let me go." "No." came her simple reply. Her skin melted away, her

eyeballs tore from her eye sockets, and her hair drifted in pieces. I shrieked, all she is, is a skeleton. A

thing of the past. Her fingers dug deeper into my hand. And I finally wrenched my arm away, "Autumn!!"

she screeched madly. Wherever she touched me it burnt and stung, like someone poured acid on it. My

heart burnt, like someone bathed it in acid. Whatever was pulling me up pulled me away, and I was in the flight again, panting for breath, as I felt my toes squish in my wet shoes.

28

Making it Through

I glimpsed down at my hands and moved my hands apart in the darkness, my left hand was clawing at the right one, in the exact same place Mom grasped me. I ran my fingers over and over the spot to calm myself. And then there was my shoes, why were they wet? I bent down to examine them and found my water bottle, strewn on the floor. Leaking everywhere, soaking my shoes, my bag. I frowned, and sighed.

Settling back. I closed my eyes. But the image of skeleton mom came to me, and my eyes flew open. I just gazed out of the window. Everything was calm. Everything was quiet. But only for a second, as usual. One crash of lightning sent me jumping in my seat. I clamped my hands together, and pressed my eyes shut.

We would make it through this flight, I scolded myself.

29

In Germany.

An announcement came through, and I was glad to hear the Captain's voice, "Hello passengers, I hope

you enjoyed your journey. Once again, thank you for choosing our airlines. Thank you." and then a

different voice in what I'm guessing is German. "Hallo passagiere, ich hoffe, sie haben ihre reise genossen.

Nochmals vielen dank, dass sie sich für unsere fluggesellschaften entschieden haben. Danke." a low

murmuring began among the flight, it bubbled and rose. I was soon on my feet, saying bye to Millie, and

collecting my suitcase. I waited at the exit for our group and I soon saw a half-asleep, half-awake, Jameson

who was stumbling more than walking. And Antonio, trying to keep him upright. I giggled at the scene,

"What?" Jameson slurred, raising his finger and pointing it in my face. "I just woke up okay?" Dad

had Bronwyn slung over his shoulders and pushed his suitcase at Jameson who stopped it with his foot.

And we carried on. We made it through the flight.

30

Confusing.

Everything in this airport was new, bustling, and confusing. Very, very confusing. There were German

signs everywhere, with a tiny English manuscript at the bottom. But it meant close to nothing because we

could barely see any of them. Our reflections gleamed on the polished marbled floors, mirroring our clear

confusion. All of us stood, staring blankly, watching the various scenes unfold in front of us. A mother was

on her phone, talking to someone, while her child tugged at her hand, pointing to a toy store. A group of

teenage girls were posing for a selfie together, while tired parents murmured between themselves. There

were then clusters of different people, friends, family, and colleagues. And I guess some people traveled

alone. "Well," Dad sighs, mustering a smile. "Are you guys ready?" "Ready," Jameson replied firmly, tugging

at his sling bag. We walked out of the airport, and a blast of cold air hit my face. I closed my eyes softly,

savoring the moment, and breathed in the fresh breeze. We walked a little further, and we despite the time there was a line of atleast 10 men. One portly, bald(ish) man leaned over the rail and said, "Hallo,

brauchen Sie ein Taxi?" he got a glimpse of the look of confusion on our faces, and rubbed it fingers

together, mumbling something. Then he looked up and said, "You need, taxi?" "Yes, yes please," Dad

replied, the man grinned a toothless grin and then beckoned for us to follow him. We walked into the

street, the stars twinkling against the night sky, I wrap my fingers around the locket, and I look up. I see. . .

I see Mom's face, smiling down at me, and I smile back up. We all get in the taxi, "Where, I take you?" the

taxi driver asks, I open my phone and type in "Nearest resort." and a four-star resort called 'The Olive

Tree.' and it doesn't seem too expensive. "Uh, The Olive Tree, please?" I ask, and with a joyful, "Ok-ayy."

the driver starts the car.

31

At last.

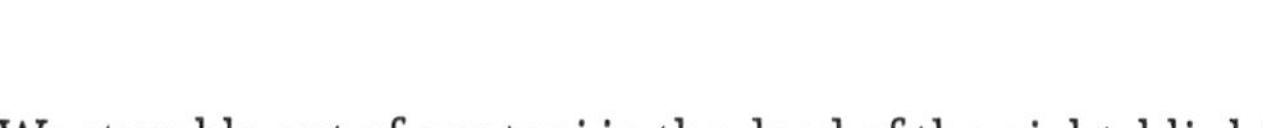

We stumble out of our taxi in the dead of the night, blinking groggily at the brightly lit sign, Dad pays

the driver and we walk inside. "Do we have enough euros for a night stay?" I croaked, "Just about enough,"

Dad murmured back. We walked inside, and we were greeted by a cheery desk attendant. "Hallo, German?

English?" she asks, "English." Dad says, "How many nights stay please?" she asks, "One night." Dad

replies, "Right this way, please." she says stepping out from behind the counter. All of us trudge behind her

in single file. We board the elevator and take it up. And we reach the 4th floor. "Alright, I will be giving

you 2 rooms, alright, room, 409, and room, 410." She says handing Jameson a key card and handing me a

key card. She beams at us and leaves. In my room, there are two single beds, its decided that me and

Bronwyn will share one, and Dad will sleep on one. Same for Antonio and Jameson. Dad takes the key

from me and swipes it swiftly, Jameson and Antonio are already in their room. "Otter?" Dad asks, "You coming?" he wears a worried expression. "Yeah, just, gimme a minute." I reply staring at my feet

intently, I feel claustrophobic in places like this. I take deep breaths, steadying myself. Two rooms away

from ours, a door clicks open, and a squat, blond man, with thinning hair steps out. He grins at me

devilishly. I recognize his face, it dawns on me. I step back, my back pressed to the door. "No," the word

escapes my lips, "No, no, no, no, how?" my feet are shaking. "Surprise." he wisps. And then I collapse.

www.ingramcontent.com/pod-product-compliance
Lightning Source LLC
La Vergne TN
LVHW091105150826
845673LV00002B/725

* 9 7 9 8 8 9 5 1 9 3 4 4 0 *